D1058366

Books by Jean Little

MINE FOR KEEPS
HOME FROM FAR
SPRING BEGINS IN MARCH
WHEN THE PIE WAS OPENED
TAKE WING
ONE TO GROW ON

One to Grow On

One to Grow On

by Jean Little

Illustrated by
Jerry Lazare

Little, Brown and Company
BOSTON   TORONTO

*Published simultaneously in Canada
by Little, Brown & Company (Canada) Limited*

PRINTED IN THE UNITED STATES OF AMERICA

For Rosemary
    with whom I would share Gilead

and for Caroline
    with whom I have shared the wrong train,
    peanut butter and poems, insults and ideas,
    bathtub plugs and boredom, argument and
    adventure, laughter and love.

Contents

1   One Sunday Morning   3

2   Hi, Lisa   12

3   Hi, Stephanie   20

4   Janie Belongs   28

5   Try Telling the Truth   37

6   Blue and Green and Gray and Gold   46

7   Yippee!   55

8   Tilly to the Rescue   61

9   Steffy Catches On   67

10   At Lisa's   73

11   "Your Brother's Home!"   81

12   Pam   89

13   Blue Lake and Rocky Shore   99

14   Dishes and Giant Steps   107

15   A Surprise and a Half   113

16   Pam Explains   120

17   Make Way for Janie   128

One to Grow On

1

One Sunday Morning

I DON'T want to go," Janie said.

Mother picked up the plastic measuring spoons Tim had just flung out of his playpen and handed them back to him politely. Tim grinned up at her and stamped his feet like a pony.

"You're quite welcome, Timothy," she told him, "but don't do it again. You're much too old for that sort of thing."

"Moth-er!" Janie's voice rose angrily.

But Mary Chisholm had moved. She was at the foot of the back stairs calling instructions up to the two teen-agers who had not yet come down.

"Elaine! Rob! If you want anything to eat this morning, you have exactly three minutes to get down here."

Janie wanted to stamp *her* foot. It was always like this, trying to talk to Mother. She was harder to catch than a diesel locomotive. Now she was plugging in the coffeepot,

turning on the tap and running the dishwater, getting out
Dad's grapefruit, pouring juice for Rob and Elaine, getting
Tim a square of toast . . .

"Stephanie Jane Chisholm," her mother said, rounding
on her suddenly and speaking in a voice edged with irrita-
tion to match Janie's own, "why must you stand right in
the middle of the floor? You couldn't be more in my way
if you tried."

"If you ever listened to me, you'd know!" Janie exploded.
"I've been trying to tell you something for *hours*. I've tried
at least *five* times — but you never hear one word."

"You've tried once. Maybe twice, Janie. And it hasn't
been 'hours.' You've been out here for only about ten minutes all told."

"It's been longer than that," Janie said weakly.

Mother shook her head. Then she began, once again,
to say the words Janie had heard so often.

"Janie, when will you learn to stop exaggerating everything so. It's time you grew up and started sticking to the
truth."

"But you *don't* listen . . ." Janie interrupted.

"I do," Mary Chisholm answered crisply. She was stack-
ing her own and Janie's breakfast dishes as she spoke. Suddenly, she looked up, hearing her husband coming down
the front stairs. Janie, catching the sound of his step an
instant later, regarded her mother with admiration. Always,
Mother heard him first.

"I am listening right now," Mother went on, picking up the grapefruit and starting in to the dining room. "I even know what it is you've been trying to tell me for 'hours' . . ."

"You don't want to go to Sunday School," she finished triumphantly, setting the half grapefruit down at her husband's place.

Dad, pulling his chair in to the table, gave her a startled glance.

"Sunday School," he echoed blankly. "Why would I want . . ."

"Don't be silly, Jim. I'm talking to Janie. She's the one who doesn't want to go to Sunday School."

"Why?" Dad asked.

Janie opened her mouth to explain but Mother beat her to it.

"Because she's the one and only person in this house who has to go — at least until Tim's a couple of years older."

Janie felt a little like a pricked balloon but she was not ready to retreat yet.

"Well, it's true," she asserted.

"Hmph," her father said and disappeared into the weekend paper.

Janie thought of telling him that he never listened either. Then she had to smile. He would not even hear her say that much. Yet, somehow, that was all right. That was just the way Dad was. She would not want him changed.

Mother was different. If Mother, just once, would pay attention . . .

Mother brought the coffeepot in and put it where her husband could reach it. Then she returned to the kitchen. Janie followed her, as determined as a bloodhound.

"There are seven people in this family," she told her mother. She spoke each word slowly, so that her mother would feel the full weight of this argument. "There's Dad and you and David and Elaine and Rob and Tim and me . . ."

"And five of us are too old for Sunday School and one is too young — and that leaves one — you!" Mother countered neatly. "Call Elaine and Rob again, will you please, dear? Tim, stop being a fire engine for a moment. I can't hear myself think. Ask Elaine if she's made her bed. No, never mind. I'll do my own asking. . . . But, speaking of beds, is yours made?"

"Yes, it is," Janie said proudly, her voice sure, her chin high.

It was so nearly true that, for an instant, she believed it herself. She *had* started to make it, after all. She had pulled the covers up and was beginning to straighten them when she had remembered it was Sunday and she had gone to find her lesson book and then, she had stopped for breakfast, and then . . .

"Good for you, Janie," Mother said warmly, giving her a real smile.

Janie squirmed. But it would be all right. She would just slip upstairs and do it before Mother learned the truth. She . . .

"Janie, I told you to call Rob and Elaine," Mother reminded her.

Elaine came clattering down.

"I'm here," she told Janie. "And my bed's made," she added to her mother. "Rob's still sleeping."

"Rob!" Janie bellowed up the back stairs.

"Okay, okay," Rob returned in a foggy voice. His feet thudded on the floor above her. "I'm coming. Tell Mom I want bacon."

Mother heard, shook her head over her son's manners, said "please" for him and opened the refrigerator door.

"Thank goodness David's not like that!" Janie exclaimed.

"Oh, David's not perfect. You've forgotten what he was like when he was Rob's age," Mother answered.

But she smiled again, just speaking David's name.

Janie understood the smile. David, at nineteen, was the eldest. That made him special. He was special, too, because he had gone away from them into a world of his own. He had just finished his first year in college and now he was in Riverside working for Andrew Copeland, a friend of Dad's, for the summer. Janie knew that her parents were proud of him. She, Janie, did not care about his good grades or the "fine experience" he was having in Riverside. She simply wanted him home where she could get to him when she needed him. David did listen.

"Nobody else is like David," she said huskily to her mother.

"Why, Janie, you and David are as alike as two peas in a pod," Mother said.

Janie stared at her.

"Me . . . like David?"

Mary Chisholm laughed. She went on putting bacon strips into the frying pan.

"When David was your age, he used to argue, for no good reason, just the way you do. And for years he's been after me to 'stop and listen'. Then, he goes off into his own thoughts and forgets the rest of us are there. You do that too. You both swoop from happiness to misery and back again in no time flat. I don't know where you get it from. Your father and I — and Elaine and Rob, too, for that matter — are so much more of a piece. You and David — I don't know what's going on inside you, half the time," Mother admitted.

Janie was fascinated.

"Did David . . ." she began eagerly.

"Did David what?" Mother probed when Janie halted in mid-sentence.

But Rob was there, all at once. And Elaine and Dad were placing their orders for bacon too.

"Nothing," Janie muttered.

She was sure, anyway, that David had not told lies when he was her age. Time was passing. Remembering her unmade bed, Janie tried to fade quietly out of sight.

"Janie, you still have twenty minutes. You could get started on those dishes," Mother said firmly.

Janie hurried but twenty minutes was not long enough.

"Heavens, Stephanie Jane, you're going to be late," Mother cried, catching sight of the clock.

She hustled Janie into hat and gloves, giving her no chance to talk. On her way to the front door, she did make one last half-hearted attempt to rebel.

"What if I just won't go?" she asked. "What if I go on strike and lie on the floor and refuse to move . . ."

"Jane Chisholm, stop talking nonsense and *hurry!*"

But before Mother had Janie safely through the door, the phone rang. Mother reached for the receiver. Janie halted, not really meaning to listen, just dawdling for a moment to show she was free to do what she pleased.

"Tilly!" Mother said happily — and Janie changed her mind about listening.

After all, Matilda Barry was Janie's godmother as well as Mother's closest friend. Tilly probably wanted to speak to her, Janie.

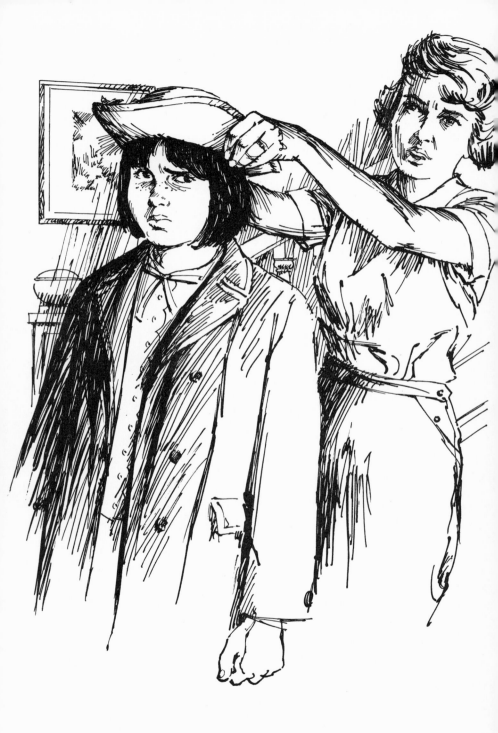

"Yes, Janie's right here — but she's on her way out the door to Sunday School and she's going to be late," Mother said.

She eyed Janie sternly as she spoke and waved "Goodbye." Janie stood her ground.

"Hold the line, for a minute, Tilly . . . Janie, go *on!*"

"But maybe Tilly . . ."

"Never you mind about Tilly. If she has any messages for you, I'll tell you at lunch. Now, march."

Janie leaned forward swiftly and spoke directly into the receiver in her mother's hand.

"Hi, Tilly."

Tilly's deep chuckle reached her.

"Hello, chicken. Didn't you hear your mother? . . . But wait till you hear about the surprise I have planned . . ."

Mother stepped back, holding Janie at arm's reach. "You bide your time, Miss Barry," she told Tilly.

Then, laying the receiver on the hall table, Mary Chisholm took a firm hold on her daughter and literally propelled her through the front door. It closed behind her with a brisk bang.

Janie was on her way to Sunday School.

2

Hi, Lisa

JANIE walked down the path to the sidewalk as slowly as she dared. She turned in the direction of the church. Then she stopped and looked around for a rock to kick along. When she found one and sent it flying down the cement, she knew that she was dulling the sheen on the toes of her Sunday shoes. She did not care.

She had known, all along, that she would have to go. She even knew, in her heart of hearts, that she liked going. Miss Andrews, her teacher, was her friend and she knew how to make the lessons come alive. But the fact that Janie liked Sunday School had nothing to do with the fact that the whole thing was unfair. Mother could say what she liked about the others' being "too old" but both she and Janie knew that there was a class for boys and girls as old as Rob and Elaine. Now they were in the choir, they claimed they were too busy. But others went to both choir and Sunday School. Mother should have made them.

Janie gave the rock an extra hard kick. It sailed out of sight into a clump of bushes. Janie halted and looked at them. She could go in after it. It would serve everyone right if she got her dress rumpled. But the bushes were full of prickles. She went on walking, leaving the rock behind.

There they all sat, she told herself, scowling fiercely — eating their bacon and talking together and laughing. There Mother stood hearing all about why Tillie had called. And here she was, all by herself, the only Chisholm going to Sunday School.

Maybe Mother had finished on the phone and was even now upstairs discovering Janie's bed unmade.

Janie pulled off her hat with a jerk and swung it in her hand. She'd show them. She shook her head wildly and her fine coppery hair flew every which way, tangling beautifully.

Janie felt better at once. Tilly never wore a hat.

"But, Till, why don't you wear a hat?" Mother had asked Tilly once in Janie's hearing.

"I can't be bothered," Tilly had answered cheerfully.

When I grow up, Janie promised herself, I'll never wear a hat either. And I'll go barefoot. And I'll take my children on a picnic some Sunday morning . . .

What was Tilly plotting? "A surprise," she had said.

Janie came out of her dream world, all at once. She looked around her. The street was perfectly quiet. Everything seemed asleep in the morning sunshine. Even the birds cheeped drowsily. There was not a soul ahead of her on the sidewalk. She *was* going to be late.

Stephanie Jane Chisholm began to run.

She was over halfway when a voice hailed her.

"Janie, how about a ride?"

Gratefully, Janie scrambled into Miss Andrews' car and fought to catch her breath.

"I thought . . . I . . . was going . . . to be late!" she puffed.

"We'll just make it by the skin of our teeth," Miss Andrews said. "I meant to start out earlier but I got involved in a crossword puzzle and I didn't notice the time. What held you up, Janie? You're usually one of the first there."

The dishes, breakfast, arguing with Mother, kicking a rock along, thinking . . . these things could not be told properly.

"My little brother was sick," Janie improvised quickly. "Mother was up with him all night and I didn't want to wake her. So I got breakfast for everybody and I just couldn't get finished in time."

As she spoke, it was very clear in Janie's mind. She saw herself tiptoeing to her mother's bedroom door, saw her mother fast asleep, her face shadowed with weariness. She pictured herself rounding up Rob and Elaine and whispering orders to them. In her mind, they obeyed her without question, their faces respectful. She was on her

way to check on Tim when Miss Andrews brought her
back to reality with a bump.

"What's wrong with Tim, Janie?"

Janie searched for something plausible. She hesitated,
but Miss Andrews was waiting.

"Measles."

"Measles," Miss Andrews repeated.

Janie sat very still. Tim had had measles at Christmas.
Why hadn't she said he had a cold? What would she say
when Miss Andrews remembered?

"Let's hope it's a light case of them," Miss Andrews said,
parking the car and turning off the motor.

She had not remembered. Janie drew a deep breath.
Then the teacher went on, "I guess we won't see your
mother in church this morning."

Janie shook her head in mute agreement. Yet not only
would Miss Andrews see Mother in church; she might very
well see Tim himself going into the Nursery — Tim all
scrubbed and shining, without a measle on him.

"I did hear Mother say maybe it wasn't really measles . . ."

Janie heard her own words stumbling wildly. "This
morning, his rash was much better or something . . . almost gone. Mother looked at breakfast . . . I mean, after
she woke up . . . Just before I left, she woke up and she
did look at him then . . ."

She was getting hopelessly lost and she knew it. At last,

she stopped and sat silently, waiting for Miss Andrews to ask her, outright, why she had lied.

"Here's a comb, Janie," Miss Andrews said gently instead. "You have about two seconds to subdue that wild mop of hair and get your hat back on. We must look our best because we're being honored with a visit from our celebrity today."

Janie looked through the window. Lisa Daniels was climbing out of her father's car and starting to go into the church. Janie hurried. She and Miss Andrews caught up with Lisa as the three of them entered the Assembly Room.

"Janie!" Lisa cried joyfully, as though she had been waiting for days for that moment to arrive.

Janie smiled shyly.

"Hi," she managed.

Lisa clutched at her elbow and gave it a squeeze. Her blue eyes shone.

"Oh, Janie, I was hoping you'd be here today," she said.

Janie wondered where else she would be on a Sunday morning. It was Lisa, not she, who rarely appeared at Sunday School.

"Girls, take your places. Dr. Howland is waiting," Miss Andrews murmured.

Lisa moved forward to the row of chairs where their class sat but she did not hurry. Lisa Daniels never hurried.

"Hi, Lisa! Hi!" the class chorused as she neared them.

Nobody gave Janie a second glance. Dr. Howland stood at the front, waiting. He cleared his throat crossly.

"I've saved you a seat, Lisa," Marlene Robinson simpered.

The chair beside Marlene was empty, but everyone knew she had not really saved it for Lisa.

"Move over, Marlene," Lisa said coolly. "I want to sit by Janie."

It was like one of Janie's daydreams. She often imagined people saying things like that.

"I want Janie for my team." "Janie is my best friend." "Janie's work is the best in the class." "Janie is the winner again!" "I want to sit by Janie."

It had never happened before. Janie sat down, looking a little dazed.

Dr. Howland read the Call to Worship and announced the first hymn. Pages of hymnbooks rustled. Lisa smiled her enchanting smile and whispered, "I've been hearing things about you, Janie Chisholm."

The piano played the opening chords. Janie, struggling to believe her ears, was saved from having to think of something to say in return as the boys and girls stood up and started to sing.

Janie sang with them but her thoughts were not on the words.

Lisa Daniels was so pretty. She had black, black hair.

It was cut short and the ends curled in softly around her
face. Summer had only just arrived in Ontario but Lisa
was still deeply tanned from the Daniels' winter holiday
in Florida. Her eyes, which should have been brown with
hair like that, were as blue as a sunny sky. Her smile left
you feeling as though you had been given a present.

What could she mean she had been "hearing things"?

"Hey, Janie, would you like me to come over to your
house this afternoon?" Lisa offered suddenly. "My parents are away all day . . ."

"Lisa, hush," Miss Andrews warned.

Lisa raised her eyebrows at Janie. Janie still felt she was
dreaming the whole thing, but she nodded her head em-
phatically all the same.

"That would be great," she added, just to make sure
Lisa understood.

Lisa turned back to her hymnary. It was settled. Janie,
who had lost her place, did not look for it. She simply
stood and tried to understand herself.

When Sunday School was over, Lisa did not stay for
church.

"See you, Janie," she called over her shoulder as she
disappeared.

Janie went to find her family. Tim had already been
left in the Nursery.

"Did you meet Miss Andrews on your way in?" Janie
wanted to know.

"No. Why?"

"Oh, I just wondered," she said lamely.

Then they were in church and it was too late to ask about Tilly's surprise or to tell Mother about Lisa.

When church was over, Janie still hugged her new secret to herself. She wanted to announce it properly. She wanted to see the whole family startled and impressed. All the way home in the car, she managed not to tell. She would wait until they were at the table.

"Mother, what did Tilly want?" she remembered to ask as they trooped into the house.

Only then did she notice the look on her mother's face.

"I believe you have something to do upstairs in your room before dinner, Janie," Mother said quietly.

Janie reddened.

"I meant . . ."

"Don't tell me what you meant to do." Mother had a note of steel in her voice.

"But if you'd just listen . . ." Janie tried bravely.

"I listened this morning," Mother said. "Now, go."

Janie went.

3

Hi, Stephanie

JANIE made her bed more carefully than usual. She mitred the corners perfectly and left not even a hint of a wrinkle. Then she picked up some of the clutter and put it away. When she changed out of her church clothes, she even put her dress on a hanger and hung it in the closet where it belonged. When she joined the family for dinner, she felt almost angelic.

When everyone had been served, she could contain herself no longer.

"Guess what?" she burst out. Then, as they looked at her blankly, she realized that there was no way they could guess and she hurried on.

"My friend Lisa is coming over this afternoon."

"What friend Lisa?" Rob asked bluntly. "You don't have any friend called Lisa."

"I do so!"

"This wouldn't be someone you've imagined, would it, Janie?" her father asked.

"The way you imagined you'd made your bed . . ." Mother started.

Then she caught sight of Janie's stricken face.

"I'm sorry, Janie," she said quickly. "Don't look like that. It's just that we've never heard you mention anyone named Lisa before."

Janie swallowed. Her great announcement had gone wrong. They were being horrible, every single one of them.

Elaine saved the day. Her eyes widened.

"You don't mean Lisa Daniels, do you?" she ventured.

"Yes," Janie said simply.

"Are you making it up?"

"Elaine!" Mother said.

She sounded shocked as though she herself had never doubted Janie's word. But Janie was only attending to her sister now.

"I'm not making it up — honest!"

"Lisa Daniels is really coming here to see you this afternoon?"

Janie nodded solemnly.

"Wow!" said Elaine.

It was the moment Janie had been waiting for. Even Dad had heard of Lisa Daniels.

"Isn't she the little girl that comes out of the toothpaste tube?" he checked.

There was a babble of talk as everyone but Tim contributed facts about Lisa and her family.

"That's the one," Mother told Dad. "She's Clare Daniels' daughter."

"Her mother's a model," Elaine breathed. Her face was wistful as she remembered Mrs. Daniels' beautiful clothes in the April *Chatelaine*.

"Her dad's Matt Daniels," Rob added. "He's a disc jockey. He does Matt's Music."

"We know, we know," Elaine said. "And Lisa does TV commercials and models for Eatons' catalog and plays the piano. What I want to know is — since when is she a friend of Janie's?"

Janie retorted too quickly, "We've been friends for ages!"

"Now, Janie," Mother warned.

"Think of a kid Janie's age having all that lovely money!" Rob said dreamily. "What time did you say she was coming?"

"She's coming to see me," Janie stated belligerently.

"Why me?" a voice inside her wondered.

"Me!" Tim yelled joyfully. "Coming see *me!*"

The Chisholms laughed but, under cover of the family uproar, Mother asked again, "What time *do* you expect her, Janie?"

"She didn't say," Janie answered uncertainly. "This afternoon sometime . . . that's all I know."

When the doorbell actually rang at two-thirty, Janie had to pinch herself to make it seem real.

Lisa swept into the Chisholm house, charming people as she came.

"A baby!" she squealed at the sight of Tim. "You're so lucky, Janie, to have a baby brother — and older brothers and sisters too. It's awful being an only child."

Janie found that hard to credit. She was glad though when Elaine came into the hall.

"Hi, Lisa," Elaine said smoothly when Janie made no attempt to introduce the two girls. "I'm Jane's sister Elaine."

"I was just telling Janie how lucky she was to be one of a big family," Lisa returned. "Being a 'one and only' is a terrible fate."

Elaine and Lisa conversed like equals. Listening to their easy talk, looking at their polite smiles, Janie thought they sounded as though they were both grown-up. Her stomach twisted nervously. Then, she took a deep breath and burst into the conversation, claiming Lisa as her guest.

"Come on up to my room," she ordered gruffly.

Lisa followed obediently.

"Don't you have another brother too?" her voice floated up to Janie, ahead of her on the stairs.

"Two," Janie said absently, wondering how they could

get off the subject of her family. "David's working in Riverside. He's just finished his first year in college."

"What about the other one?" Lisa wanted to know, as Janie opened her bedroom door and stood back to let the other girl go in first.

"The other . . ." Janie was puzzled for a moment. "Oh, my other brother. Rob's fifteen. He's awful!"

"Really?" Lisa was clearly waiting for more.

What else was there to say about Rob? Janie wondered helplessly. He was fifteen, he was her brother and he was awful.

"I guess he's not really so bad," she put in, her loyalty a little late. "He's just like all brothers. Except Tim, of course. And David's okay too when he's home."

Suddenly, overwhelmingly, she missed her brother David. If only he were home to share her excitement over Lisa's coming. David would have known, from the beginning, that Janie was telling the truth about Lisa. The truth came more easily, somehow, when David was there.

"Where is he this afternoon?" Lisa asked idly.

"I told you, he's in Riverside . . . oh, you mean Rob," she corrected herself, reading her mistake on Lisa's face. "Who knows? Probably listening to his records. He's always playing his records. He built himself a hi-fi."

"He did!" Lisa was obviously impressed.

But Janie had had enough of Rob. She wanted Lisa to

know her, Janie, to like her because she was herself, not because she was part of her family.

She sat very still for an instant, staring at Lisa, trying to make up her mind. Then, clutching at her courage, she began.

"Lisa . . ." Janie's voice was unsteady with excitement — and with fear that Lisa would laugh. Lisa's attention was caught at last.

"What is it?" she asked, as Janie hesitated.

"Lisa, would you call me Stephanie?" Janie begged, all in a rush. "That's my first name, Stephanie, and I've always wanted someone to call me by it but I never told anyone before. I'm so sick of being called Janie. Janie's a baby name, if you ask me."

Lisa almost laughed. Then the intense longing on Janie's face sobered her.

"Sure," she said kindly, speaking in the same voice Mother used when she reassured Tim. "I'll call you Stephanie, if you want. Hi, Stephanie!"

Then she did laugh — and Janie laughed with her. She collapsed onto the bed at Lisa's side. She giggled wildly.

"What sort of records does your brother like, Stephanie?" Lisa asked then.

"All kinds," Janie said, still laughing.

It was wonderful, she thought. She felt different already, like a completely new person.

"I'm Stephanie," she thought proudly. "And Lisa Daniels is my friend."

She had begun to believe it.

4

Janie Belongs

LISA stayed for supper.

Janie had enjoyed the afternoon. She and Lisa had lain on her bed and talked much of the time. Janie confided her longing for a bicycle, her problems with Elaine, her ideas on how to avoid Sunday School, her admiration of Miss Andrews. This was the way Janie imagined friendship being, having someone to share things with, someone who really listened, someone who cared about important things. Once or twice, Lisa said "Yes" when she should have said "No," and Janie wondered, for a fleeting instant, if the other girl were really listening. But then, Lisa, catching sight of Janie's face, would correct herself swiftly and smile her lovely smile — and Janie would talk on.

Lisa talked too. When Janie pressed her for details about her life as a model and an actress, she gave them.

She spoke of her parents, at Janie's insistence. Janie was wide-eyed with wonder when Lisa announced that her father wrote popular songs.

"He wrote 'A Fistful of Love' and 'Walk Me to the Corner,' " Lisa said. "He composes under a different name and he doesn't talk about it much but he's very good."

"Rob has both those records," Janie breathed. "He just loves 'Walk Me to the Corner.' Wait till I tell him . . ."

Lisa, who had been beginning to sound sleepy, roused suddenly. She wanted to know what other records Rob liked, when his birthday was, whether he went steady with anyone, whether he liked girls.

Janie sighed and told all she knew about her brother Rob. What she did not know, she invented. According to Janie, Rob hated all girls but no less than three of them were fighting over him, tooth and nail. His favorite color was blue, she told Lisa. He wanted to be a pilot when he got out of school.

"My favorite color's blue too," Lisa smiled to herself.

When Janie finally ran out of things to tell about Rob, Lisa went on to question her about David, and then Elaine. When they reached Elaine, Janie balked and suggested they watch television. At five-thirty, Mother came in and asked if Lisa would like to stay for supper.

"I'd be delighted, Mrs. Chisholm," Lisa said prettily. "Could I phone our housekeeper and ask?"

"Your housekeeper?" Mother echoed.

"Yes, my parents are visiting friends in Hamilton and I'm supposed to be spending the day with Mrs. Wallace. I did tell her I was going out but I didn't tell her where I'd be," Lisa said.

Mrs. Wallace was upset when Lisa phoned. From across the room, Janie could hear her voice crackling into Lisa's ear. But Lisa had her way and stayed.

At the supper table, she was the center of attention. Once again, she was questioned about her work. This time, her account sparkled. She told funny little stories about mishaps at the TV studio. She made faces of pretended disgust as she told them all of how she had started modeling when she was a "fat baby" and of how her mother kept a scrapbook of her appearances in magazines.

"She even has one when I was advertising a lotion for diaper rash," Lisa shuddered. "It is horrible!"

Rob roared with laughter. Janie laughed too. Nobody could have helped it. Lisa told it so well, so wittily. Suddenly, studying the enchanted faces of her family, Janie wanted to remind them that this dazzling creature they were enjoying so was her friend, that it was she, Janie, whom Lisa was visiting. But nobody was noticing Janie at all. Even Dad was wholly taken up with the guest.

"Lisa, your supper's getting cold," Mother said all at once. "We're not giving you a chance to eat with our questions. You go ahead and eat right now. And the rest of you, leave her be till she catches up. I have some news for you all anyway, especially Janie."

Lisa gave Mother a measuring glance. Janie had a queer feeling that Lisa did not like being told to eat while Mother talked. But, after a second, she did begin on her meat pie.

"Tilly called this morning," Mother said.

Janie gasped. How could she have forgotten? Questions came from everywhere like a swarm of bees.

"What did she say?" "Is she coming to stay?" "Why didn't you tell us?"

"Matilda Barry is a friend of mine," Mother explained to Lisa. "And she's Janie's godmother."

"She's an artist," Elaine chimed in. "She did those portraits of us behind you."

Lisa swiveled around on her chair and looked where Elaine was pointing.

"She hasn't done Tim yet," Elaine went on. "She's waiting for him to grow old enough to sit still."

"That'll be the day," Rob commented, giving Tim a friendly poke.

"Who's that?" Lisa asked.

Janie stiffened. She had known Lisa would ask. Elaine and Rob were so obviously Elaine and Rob. David's picture was in the living room. That left only one.

"That's Tilly's Janie," Mother said quietly. "Janie was

much younger then, of course. I think she was seven, weren't you?"

Janie nodded. She knew what Lisa was thinking. Then Lisa said it.

"I've never seen Janie look like that."

Mother studied the picture in silence as though she were seeing it for the first time all over again. Tilly had drawn Janie sitting by a window looking out over a snowy garden. On the windowsill was a small gray bird, eating daintily. And on the face of the child watching him was a grave beauty, a shining tenderness. It was a very private and special picture.

"Don't talk to me about this one," Tilly had said gruffly when she dumped the big, clumsily wrapped package in Mother's lap. Mother had taken off the wrappings and held up the painting and looked at it. Then, suddenly, without making a sound, she had begun to cry. Janie had never forgotten the strangeness of that moment nor the way Tilly, who rarely kissed anyone, had leaned down and kissed Mary Chisholm on the cheek.

"I have seen her look like that," Mother said now, "but only on rare occasions. I think, though, that Tilly sees her that way nearly all the time."

Janie shied away from the wistful sound in the words and from the open doubt on Lisa's face.

"You still haven't told us what Tilly wanted," Dad said then.

"Oh, yes," Mother remembered. "She's coming for Janie on Saturday morning to take her on an 'expedition.' She wouldn't tell me why or where they would be going. But she did say, if everything worked out, there'd be a surprise for all of us at the finish."

"Maybe she's taking Janie shopping for a birthday present," Elaine suggested.

"Six weeks ahead of time?" Mother was doubtful. "She said not to expect her if it rains. If it's a summery day, she'll be here to pick you up at ten."

"Didn't she invite anyone but Janie?" Elaine asked.

"Who else is there?" Janie said pertly.

She herself had thought of her birthday hopefully, but Mother was right. You wouldn't need to buy a bicycle six weeks early.

Then it was time for Lisa to go. Janie stood watching her get her jacket on. She felt forlorn. The wonderful afternoon was so abruptly over. And tomorrow would be just like all the other days.

"I'll be by in the morning to call for you, Janie," Lisa said. Then she dimpled at the rest of the family. " 'Bye, everybody. Good-bye, Rob. I'll be seeing you."

Janie stared after her. Then, coming to her senses, she called, "Sure, Lisa. I'll be ready."

Lisa always came to school with Martha Jefferson and Jo Martin. . . . No, that was before. Lately, she was friends with Pam Potter and Debbie Wellington. Janie

checked back in her memory. Yes, Pam and Debbie were
the latest. There had been a time when it had been Martha
and Jo and a time before that when Suzie Black and Gay
Hoffman had always been with her. Always Lisa had been
at the center, shining, sure of herself, laughing, and the
others had followed along, knowing how lucky they were.
Was this the way those friendships had started? Was Lisa
really going to walk with her, Janie, in the morning instead of with Debbie and Pam? Janie felt as startled as
Alice when she fell into Wonderland. She was just as
unsure what would happen next.

When the Chisholms' doorbell rang at eight-thirty,
Janie found all three girls on the step, waiting. Debbie
and Pam looked uncertain too. Unable to think of a word
to say, Janie grabbed her books and joined them.

"I don't think you girls know each other," Lisa said
teasingly as they went down the path to the sidewalk. She
was ahead, her arm linked in Debbie's.

Janie, trying to get used to the fact that she was walking to school with three other girls instead of speeding
along by herself, did not understand at first. Of course she
knew Pam and Debbie. They had never been friends, but
all four of them had been in the same class at school all
year.

"This is Debbie Wellington and Pam Potter," Lisa in-
troduced them, "And that is Stephanie Chisholm."

Lisa's voice was mocking. Janie gulped, felt foolish,

tried to find something clever to say, but remained uncomfortably silent.

"Stephanie," the other two echoed.

"We mustn't call her 'Janie.' It's a 'baby name.' " Lisa quoted Janie's own words.

Janie remembered having said them. They had sounded all right at the time. Now, as Lisa repeated them, they sounded silly even to Janie.

"It *is* a baby name," she defended herself weakly. "And Stephanie is my real first name."

"Stephanie is awfully long." Debbie looked sideways at Janie's troubled face. "I vote we call her Steffy for short."

"Steffy it is," Lisa agreed. Then she leaned close to Debbie and whispered something.

Janie's sharp ears caught the words "How about 'Stuffy'?"

But Lisa was her friend. Janie's hearing must have played a trick on her, she was sure. If Lisa felt that way, why would she have offered to call for Janie? Why had she suggested coming over the afternoon before? It didn't make sense.

"Steffy, what are you making your speech about?" Lisa asked lightly.

Janie looked at her. Lisa glanced back and smiled. Her smile was as gay and friendly as ever.

"Elizabeth Barrett Browning," Janie said slowly. Then, as she thought about it, her voice took on life and sparkle.

"She's a poet. David told me about her. Have you ever read this book?"

She held out her library book *The Silver Chord* for them to see.

"David said I'd like it and I did. It's a love story really. Elizabeth Barrett lives in this awful house with her terrible father. . . ."

Janie was off. Lisa barely glanced at the book, but at the magic words "love story," interest kindled in her face.

"So they ran away to Italy." Janie was still talking when they reached the school.

She finished at the classroom door. As the four of them swept into their "home room," Janie was suddenly completely happy, right down to her toes. She was one of them, part of Lisa Daniels' gang, accepted, popular, exciting. She, Janie Chisholm, had arrived.

5

Try Telling the Truth

"JANIE, you got some mail this morning," Mother said on Wednesday noon.

Dear Janie,
    The surprise is blue, green, gray and gold. It's bigger than a bread-box and smaller than South America.
    See you Saturday, love to all,   Tilly

Janie read it once and then again. What on earth was blue and green and gray and gold?

"Listen, everybody," she called, and she read Tilly's message aloud.

"She's crazy!" Elaine said. Then she added, honestly, "But I can hardly wait to find out what she's talking about. You're lucky, Janie. Aunt Eileen never takes me on expeditions like that."

"And Tilly never gives Janie clothes or takes her to fashion shows," Mother reminded Elaine. "I think we did pretty well when we chose godparents for you. Rob's the only one who gets neglected. Dick and Susan are so far away in New Zealand that they've forgotten all about him."

"Lisa doesn't have a godmother," Janie said thoughtfully.

"Lisa's mother wasn't an Anglican before she was married, I suspect."

"Lisa says Anglicans are Episcopalians."

"That's what they call them in the United States," Mother agreed. "How did Lisa get to be such an authority?"

"I don't know," Janie said. "We were just talking."

Lisa had made her uncomfortable when they had talked about godparents and Anglicans. But, with Tilly's postcard in her hand, it was hard for Janie to think of Lisa.

". . . Bigger than a bread-box," she mused. "It could be anything."

On Thursday afternoon after school, Janie walked down the hall at a snail's pace. Maybe if she took long enough, Pam Potter would give up waiting and go on without her. Why Lisa bothered with Pam, Janie could not understand. Pam was a heavy-set girl who moved slowly and smiled seldom. Although the two girls had walked to and from school together for four days now, Pam had not yet spoken directly to Janie. When she did say something, she said it to Lisa. And now, Janie was stuck with her.

Janie shouldered open the school door and spotted Pam at once. Neither girl called a greeting. When Janie reached her, though, Pam spoke first.

"Where's Lisa?"

"She and Debbie have to stay in for extra help with their Math. She's furious. She told Mr. Marriott she understood how to do the problems but she was away when we took that new stuff, and Debbie missed half the questions on the test. I said we'd wait for them but Lisa said he takes ages and ages explaining and we should go ahead."

Pam turned and started down the walk. Her shoulders were slumped, her head down. Janie followed.

"I suppose you believed every word of that, didn't you?" Pam said scornfully, all at once.

Janie stopped in her tracks and stared at the other girl.

"Why shouldn't I?" she asked sharply, ready to spring to Lisa's defense.

Pam kept on walking so that Janie had to scurry after her.

"Remember how we exchanged papers and marked each

other's after the test," she said. "I marked Debbie's. She got every answer right."

"But Lisa told me . . ." Janie's protest faltered into silence.

Lisa must have told her a lie. Perhaps it had been a mistake, she thought, seeing Lisa's bright face, hearing Lisa's voice saying "Debbie and I are so *mad!*" No, that could not have been a mistake. Janie struggled with the truth, trying to make it fit her picture of Lisa.

"They just didn't want to walk with us, that's all," Pam said dully. "They've done it to me before."

"Maybe they had something private to discuss . . . or something," Janie offered lamely.

How could Lisa! How could she! Janie's thoughts ran around and around in a maddening circle. Which Lisa was real? Why did Lisa bother to lie to her?

"See you tomorrow," Pam said — and Janie realized that they were at her own front door. They had come most of the way in silence.

She repeated "Tomorrow . . ."

"Sure," Pam said, lifelessly. "They'll pick us up tomorrow as though nothing had happened. So long."

Janie trailed into the house.

"How was school?" Mother asked.

Janie scowled. Every day, every single solitary day, her mother asked the same question in the same words.

"Okay, I guess," Janie returned.

Her mother sighed as though she, too, were tired of their daily exchange. But she went on, "Did you walk home with Lisa and the other girls?"

"Yes," Janie told her glibly. "I walked with Lisa really. Debbie and Pam just came along. They're always trying to shove in between me and Lisa but Lisa likes me the best."

"Janie, are you sure that's the way it really is?" her mother questioned.

"Of course I'm sure." Janie felt her cheeks growing hot under her mother's gaze. "Lisa said to me today that they were pests but she's too kind-hearted to drop them. She *did*, Mother. You don't need to look at me like that. You can ask Lisa and see for yourself."

Her stomach gave a sickening lurch as she heard her own last words. But Mother never would ask Lisa.

"Set the table for supper, will you, before you go upstairs," Mother said. "I want to get Tim fed and off to bed. He didn't nap this afternoon and he's as cranky as a bear."

Janie, getting out the knives and forks, tried to concentrate her thoughts on Tilly's coming and what it meant, on Elizabeth Barrett Browning, on how she missed David, on anything but Lisa's lie and her own. It was impossible. Much as she loved Tilly and David, curious as she was about Tilly's plans for Saturday, interested as she was in

Elizabeth Barrett's life, she kept losing her hold on them.

Why? pounded inside her head, over and over again. She was not sure whether it was herself or Lisa she could not understand.

"Janie Chisholm, don't you even know how to set a table properly after all these years?" Elaine's voice cut through the hammering and rescued her. She looked down. Sure enough, the spoons were on the wrong side and she'd given everyone two knives.

She opened her mouth to put Elaine in her place — and then she laughed instead.

"I always eat my soup with two knives," she said.

"And your pie with a spoon, I suppose," Elaine commented. But, to Janie's surprise, she helped straighten out the cutlery and even put on the salt and pepper shakers, which Janie invariably forgot.

She began to sing under her breath as they worked together.

> *"Walk me to the corner.*
> *Walk me 'round the block.*
> *Walk me to the bus stop*
> *Walk with me and talk.*
> *Walk me to forever*
> *Where we need never part.*
> *Walk me to the corner.*
> *Walk me to your heart."*

"You know what," Janie said excitedly, remembering. "Lisa's father wrote that song."

"He did not," Rob said, coming in just in time to catch the last of Elaine's song. "Joey Hallam wrote it."

"He did not!" Janie said hotly. Then she recalled Lisa's exact words and changed her story. "Well, maybe that *is* the name. Lisa said her father used a different name when he wrote music. But he wrote that and another one, too, that you like. I can't remember . . ."

"Look, Stephanie Jane," Rob said, in a patient big brother voice. "You don't have to sell me on Matt Daniels. I think he's great already. And Lisa's an okay little kid. I wouldn't mind having a sister like that instead of the two I'm stuck with. But try telling the truth for once. I saw Joey Hallam play and sing 'Walk Me to the Corner' on TV just last week and he told about how he came to write it. And it *wasn't* Mr. Daniels in disguise either. Honestly, some of the stuff you spout and expect us to swallow! It beats me!"

Janie backed away from him, her eyes snapping with fury. Why, she *was* telling him the truth. Lisa had said herself . . .

Lisa . . . Lisa had lied again. Not Janie, Lisa.

"I didn't lie. I'm *not* making up any of it," she began.

But the words which should have burst out of her, sparking with righteous anger, came out weak and unsure, as though she *were* lying.

"Forget it," Rob advised her now. "But, just for a change and a rest, try the truth one of these days and see how you like it."

He went clattering out of the room and up the stairs.

"We're done, Janie," Elaine said. There was a softness in her voice.

She's sorry, Janie thought.

Then she looked at Elaine and understood. Elaine was sorry because she thought Janie had been caught lying. Elaine had not wondered, even for a moment, whether the story might have started with Lisa.

The doorbell rang.

"Janie, there's the paper boy. Pay him, will you?" Mother called.

Janie had to clear her throat before she could call back "Okay," and go to get the money from the kitchen purse.

6

Blue and Green and Gray and Gold

"B UT I still don't know where we're going!" Janie
said as she and Tilly, in Tilly's little car, swung
into the traffic.

"I know you don't," Tilly laughed. "I thought I'd let
the family stew awhile longer. They were so curious it
was funny. And I want to see if you and I are as much
alike as I think we are."

"How do you mean?" Janie wanted to know.

She curled her feet under her and half-turned to look
at her godmother. She felt so comfortable, so at ease with
Tilly. She and Tilly fitted together, belonged, just as she
and David did. It was a feeling she rarely had with the
rest of her family. She did not lie to Tilly.

"Right beside you, on the seat, there's a page out of the

newspaper," Tilly explained. "I want you to take it and
read it over and tell me, if you were going to investigate
one of those ads, which one would it be?"

Janie pounced on the paper and scanned it quickly. It
was a page listing SUMMER COTTAGES AND PROPERTIES
FOR SALE AND RENT.

"Oh, Tilly, are you going to rent a cottage?"

"Don't ask questions, child. Read," Tilly said sternly.

Janie began at the top and worked her way down. There
were cottages with sun decks and boats, cottages with fire-
places and good fishing, cottages with indoor plumbing
and easy access to stores. They all sounded wonderful to
Janie but no one ad looked special. She read on.

She was in the PROPERTY FOR SALE when she found
one.

FOR SALE: Point with small private island. 700′ of
shoreline, Call Muskoka . . .

Small private island! There was nothing about fishing or
swimming, sun decks or boathouses. Maybe Tilly did not
feel the way she did about islands. "Small private island."
It sounded like a special place where a girl could go alone
and explore and dream and read, perhaps . . .

"Janie, don't just sit there," Tilly laughed. "Tell me
what's taken your fancy."

Janie still hesitated. It was such a little ad.

"Janie," Tilly warned. "I'm going to explode."

"Point and small private island . . ." Janie read out slowly.

"That's my girl," said Tilly exultantly. "I knew you'd know a good thing when you saw it. Not that I'm sure it is, mind you. I've marked a couple of others down. We can look at them too. But I want a place where I can take myself and my goddaughter for a holiday. This being a godmother is a serious business, you know. I'm supposed to make sure you're having a proper spiritual upbringing. I think the best way to do it is to take a hand in it myself."

"Oh, Tilly," Janie said. She settled back with a sigh of contentment. She did not even mourn over the bicycle she had pictured so longingly. A point in Muskoka with a small private island!

"Blue and green and gray and gold . . ."

They stopped at the other places first. One looked like a city house transplanted by a lake. It had a patio and a little, neat lawn. Tilly and Janie were scornful when they got back in the car. The other was perched on high rocks. The setting was lovely but the cottage was dingy and cramped. It was painted a mud brown and the two of them left it behind gladly.

Then they were getting close to the point. "THREE MILE LAKE" read a sign.

"We must be nearly there," Tilly said. She sounded every bit as excited as Janie.

But first they had to find the man who owned the property. It seemed to Janie to take hours. They finally found his farm. As the little car turned into the lane that wound up to the house, Tilly said, "Janie, remember we may not like it at all. And right now, we must start sounding practical and sensible. Tell yourself it won't be right for us. If it isn't, we'll look again. There are other little islands, I'm sure of that."

Mr. Hollis shook Janie's hand as though she were an adult.

"So you want to see the Point," he smiled at the two of them. "I'll come along and show it to you myself. My wife and I think it's the prettiest point in Muskoka."

Janie tried to act sensible, but her eyes danced and her mouth quirked up at the corners in spite of her. As Mr. Hollis went ahead in his car, Tilly reached out her hand and gave Janie's fist an understanding squeeze.

They followed a road which twisted through the Muskoka bush. Silver birches leaned out of the forest of darker trees. Great rocks jutted up on either side of them. Then, suddenly, there would be a glimpse of blue water, a gleaming stretch of lake. Tilly began to sing softly and Janie joined in.

> *"Land of the silver birch, home of the beaver,*
> *Where still the mighty moose wanders at will,*
> *Blue lake and rocky shore,*

I will return once more . . .
Boom-di-di-oom-boom . . ."

The song stopped abruptly as they came over a rise in the dirt road and found themselves perched at the top of a hill so steep the road seemed to fall away from them.

"He said the Point was at the foot of a steep hill," Tilly told Jane unnecessarily, as they inched down.

And there it was to their right.

All her life, Janie was to remember the way the Point looked that first evening when she and Tilly discovered it.

The sun was about to set and the sky was filled with golden light. They climbed out of their cars and just stood. Mr. Hollis felt the same as they did, Janie could tell, for he did not make a sound.

They were standing on top of the ridge which formed the Point. All around them, jack pines soared up into the sky. There was a soft sighing of wind in the trees and a rustle of birds and small animals. It was such a gentle sound it made the silence around them bigger. The golden light, spilling through the tall, tall tree trunks, made Janie feel as though she were in a church, except that it was lovelier there than at any man-made church she had visited.

Mr. Hollis cleared his throat and said in a voice not much louder than a whisper, "Look around all you like. You can't really see it till you've walked around it. If you've any questions, I'll be glad to answer them."

Tilly took Janie's hand and they started out. Mr. Hollis followed. They found their way down from the high hill to the water's edge. There were a hundred special places there, on the great shelving rocks, where people could lie in the sun or sit and read or have a picnic. They went on further. Janie was holding her breath now. She knew it must be just down here at the tip of the Point, just beyond these trees . . . and then, she saw it.

The island was exactly Janie's size. It was not big enough for a house, but it had a handful of trees, rocks for sitting on, a look of being a separate land, an undiscovered private place. A strip of shallow water, about twenty feet across, separated it from the mainland.

"Oh . . ." Janie breathed.

"Go ahead," Tilly said gently. "Take off your shoes and go on while I talk to Mr. Hollis."

Janie had no word to say. She sat down, pulled off her shoes and socks and stepped into the water. It was over her knees but not too much. She held her skirt up out of harm's way. She had to go carefully because of the rocks on the bottom. She tried to see them through the water. Then, she found the water growing shallower and she was clambering out onto the rocks.

Tilly had taken Mr. Hollis back the way they had come. Janie could only faintly hear their voices. Then she could not hear them at all. She wandered over the tiny island. It seemed to her as though it knew she was there, as though it was glad she had come at last, as though it had perhaps been there waiting for her for hundreds of years.

She sat down on the top of the biggest rock of all, with her back to the Point. She might have been far out to sea. She could see the far shore, of course, drowsing in a golden haze. But there was no sound of human habitation anywhere.

Whether Tilly bought it or not, whether she, Janie, ever came again, this island would always be hers, put away safely in the secret places in her heart. She wanted to do something, say something, to mark the moment. She thought about it, sitting so still she was like a part of the rock on which she perched. Then, she began to sing, very softly,

> *"Day is done.*
> *Gone the sun*
> *From the lakes, from the hills, from the sky.*
> *All is well.*
> *Safely rest.*
> *God is nigh."*

She had known Taps ever since she was a little girl and Elaine had come home from Explorers singing it. But it had never meant anything out of the ordinary until that moment. The sun had gone now. The air was cooling around her. But still, the sky was touched with light.

She stood up.

"Safely rest," she whispered once more to her own little island.

Then, she left it and started back to find Tilly.

7

Yippee!

TILLY did not ask: "How was the island?"
She took one look at Janie's rapt face and simply said, "As wonderful as that. Get your shoes on. Mr. Hollis and I have finished our discussion. I'll let you know in the next day or two, Mr. Hollis. Is it all right if Janie and I stay here now and have a picnic before we go?"

"Of course. That's fine," Mr. Hollis said, heartily.

A picnic! Janie's eyes glowed. How did Tilly always know exactly what she was wanting? She had had no idea that Tilly had brought along a picnic. But her godmother produced sandwiches, lemonade and bananas from the back of the car and led the way down to the rocks at the water's edge.

"There's no cottage, Janie. You realize that," she said, as they bit into their first sandwich.

Janie nodded and waited.

"He says there's wonderful fishing . . . but I don't fish," Tilly mused. "There's that shallow place where you waded across. Tim could go in safely there — if we were to buy. And right here, you can dive in. There's room enough for me to paint without having someone breathing down my neck every minute . . . But it costs more than I'd bargained for."

Janie chewed and listened. Tilly laughed.

"You don't say much, do you, miss," she teased. "But you argue better than you know. When I picked you up today, you had such a worried, citified look, as though you were carrying the weight of the world . . . and now, you look as though the world was your Yo-Yo. You're the real, underneath Janie I love."

Janie nearly dropped her sandwich.

"Worried . . ." she echoed.

Then she remembered the moment when Tilly had walked in. Lisa had just called. She had wanted to come over for the afternoon. Janie had told her she was going away.

"Oh well," Lisa had said lightly, "I can always go to Debbie's. But sometimes, she bores me."

Then she had invited Janie to come over to her house overnight next Friday. Janie had felt her heart leap with pleasure at the news that Debbie bored Lisa. But as swift as her pleasure came a sudden hurtful knowledge that Lisa had said such a thing about her friend. And what

about the song Lisa had claimed her father wrote? And
what about Pam?

"I'd love to come," Janie had said quickly.

But as she hung up the receiver and turned to welcome
Tilly, her face had been clouded with small nagging
doubts. And Tilly had seen, in that instant, and understood.

"What is the trouble, Janie," Tilly asked now, gently,
"or is it something you can't talk about?"

"I don't know," Janie said unhappily. "I guess . . . it's
Lisa."

Her voice slowed as she spoke Lisa's name.

Tilly held out a banana and listened.

Janie explained who Lisa was. The words did not come
easily at first, but soon, she was remembering all of it for
Tilly — that morning only a week ago when Lisa had
come to Sunday School, the first afternoon, the week of
walking to school together, the little things that hurt,
Lisa's way of walking first with one and then another,
whispering secrets, and, finally, Lisa's lies.

She thought she was done, but then, surprising herself
as much as Tilly, she discovered much more to tell. She
was always in the wrong at home and she did not know
why. Mother, Dad, Rob and Elaine all thought Lisa was
so wonderful. And Lisa was wonderful. Janie still thought
so — most of the time. But . . . but . . .

"It's the lies she tells," she ended miserably. "I know I

tell lies too. But Lisa's . . . I shouldn't mind Lisa's doing it when I do it. I never mean to lie, Tilly. It just seems to happen before I know I'm going to. Lisa's, though, seem different somehow. Worse. But that's awful. Maybe she can't help it either."

Tilly put her banana peelings away carefully before she answered.

"It's such a tangle, Janie," she said at last, speaking thoughtfully. "You're going to have to work it out for yourself. But you should perhaps think about two things. There must be a reason why you tell lies sometimes and why Lisa does too. I think I can guess why you do. You're often a fish out of water at home. You say that yourself. You're younger than the rest, and yet, so much older than Tim. We all want someone to pay attention to us, to see how special and interesting we are. When you're with your parents and Rob and Elaine, I think maybe you feel not special enough and you try to make up a different person you think they'll pay more attention to. Did you ever notice, Janie, that you tell the truth without thinking about it whenever you are with me or with David?"

Janie had known this but she had never stopped to ask herself why.

"David and I talked about it once. I think most of the lies you tell are like 'dress-up clothes.' You try them on to make a different impression. One of these days, Janie, you won't need to deck yourself out in them any longer.

You'll discover how interesting the real, true you is, just as she stands. You probably don't believe me — but you will. You'll also come to realize how much easier it is to tell the truth and how fascinating truth can be. Who'd believe you and I would be up here having a picnic on our own point in Muskoka tonight — and yet, here we are. You won't need to make a different story out of it when you get home. It's fun as it is."

Janie nodded. She thought she knew what Tilly meant, but that did not solve the problem of Lisa.

"As for Lisa," Tilly said, as though she could read Janie's mind. "I think her lies *are* different, from what you've said. Maybe Lisa needs to feel her friends depend entirely on her. I don't know Lisa. I'm just guessing. But I'd go carefully if I were you, Janie. Lisa can be cruel, it seems. Try to remember that there are other friends ahead of you. Not that that is any comfort at all, right now, I know."

She got up and looked around her. Evening had come now. It was so still. The sun had dropped and the lake reflected the first stars like a giant mirror. Suddenly, from across the lake, a loon laughed.

"Oh, Janie," Tilly said suddenly, "I love this place already. You and I'll bring a tent until I can get a cottage built. How much longer till school's finished?"

"Three weeks," Janie squeaked, jumping up and staring, wide-eyed, at her godmother's excited face.

"I won't wait till tomorrow," Tilly said, reaching for Janie and giving her a hug. "We'll stop at Mr. Hollis' right now and tell him we must have it."

"Yippee!" Janie yelled, whirling around, tripping on a ledge of rock, and sprawling onto the ground.

"Did you hurt yourself, Janie?" Tilly cried.

Janie did not bother to answer. She just stared up at the great, beautiful sky above her and yelled again, "Yippee!"

8

Tilly to the Rescue

"I THINK, perhaps, I won't come in, Janie," Tilly said, as she halted the little car in front of the Chisholms' house. "It *is* getting late and I have to get back to North York tonight. Besides, I'd like you to have the fun of telling them yourself."

"No, Tilly," Janie's voice rose in alarm. She clutched at her godmother's arm. "You have to come in and tell them. They won't believe just me."

Tilly looked down at the earnest face beside her. Her lips set suddenly.

"Oh, they won't, won't they," she said grimly. Then she patted Janie's hand and went on in her ordinary voice. "Well, I didn't want to leave anyway. I'm dying to see your parents' faces when they hear what mad Matilda Barry has done now. Move, Janie."

Janie scrambled out of the car and ran for the house.

"Here they are!" Mother called to the rest, meeting them in the hall. Chisholms assembled from all directions. Only Tim, asleep in his crib, was missing. Their eyes were fixed on Tilly's face. Tilly simply smiled at them and led the way to the living room. The questions were flying long before they had each found a chair. Janie, for greater safety and support, sat cross-legged on the floor at her godmother's feet.

"Tell us, Tilly. We've been dying of curiosity all day," Mother said.

"What did you take Janie for?" Elaine wanted to know, envy plain in her voice. "Was it something for her?"

"They probably just had a picnic," Dad guessed, looking at their empty hands.

"Picnic nothing," Rob jeered. "Look at their faces. They look like . . . like . . ."

"Like Tim when he's been into my cupboards while my back was turned," Mother laughed. "Till, don't be so mean. Tell us."

"Why ask me?" Tilly countered. "Janie was there. She can tell you the whole story."

"Let's not have Janie's version," Rob answered, only half-teasing. "I'd like to know what really happened."

"Rob, hush," Mother told him. She turned to Janie then.

"What happened, dear?" she said.

Janie savored her importance for one long, silent moment. They were all just sitting there, watching her, waiting for her to speak.

"Tilly bought an island!" she burst out then, "and a point," she added.

There was an immediate uproar.

"An island! Where?"

"A point . . . land? Oh Till, you didn't . . . did you?"

"Where? You mean, a real island . . . a body of land entirely surrounded by water?" Rob wanted to be sure.

"Go on, Janie. Tell them the whole story," Tilly said quietly.

They were on the edges of their chairs now but they hushed finally and waited for more.

Janie started at the beginning. As she told, step by step, of the wonderful day, she remembered Tilly telling her how "fascinating" the truth could be. Tilly had been right. She, Janie, did not need to add to the truth this time. It was perfect just as it had really happened.

But the other Chisholms kept interrupting. Over and over, they asked "Did you really, Tilly?" "Is that true, Tilly?"

When Janie told about the two of them going back to see Mr. Hollis and recounted the way Tilly had announced, "I'll buy your point and island, Mr. Hollis. I'm not sure where the money will come from but I'll find it. My goddaughter needs that island for personal and private reasons and I intend she should have it." Even Mother was doubtful.

"Till, what did you really tell the man?" she said, "Janie's story is all very well, fantastic in fact, but what actually went on?"

"We know our Janie too well, I'm afraid," Dad backed Mother up. He smiled at Janie as he said it but he continued. "She likes to embroider the truth. We count on her to entertain us. But this time we want the facts . . . You understand, don't you, Janie?"

Janie stared at her parents. She was telling the truth. She had not said one untrue word. A sob pushed up into her throat suddenly, and she could not manage speech. She swallowed desperately and tried to understand what was happening to her.

Then Tilly exploded.

"It so happens," she said, her tone icy, "that Janie has not lied. She has not even exaggerated. She has remembered details I would not have thought of and has told you about our afternoon better than I could have. Yet, from the moment we arrived, from the moment we stepped inside that door, every one of you has been expecting her to lie. Every one of you has been sure, positive, absolutely certain, you could not trust this child. If I were Janie, I'd lie too. Or I just would not ever tell any of you anything. I suppose Rob and Elaine have told the truth, the whole truth and nothing but the truth all their lives. That is

something *I* don't believe! As for you, Mary, I can remember more than once when you . . . shall we say
. . . 'dramatized' the truth a bit? Oh, the lot of you make
me sick and tired."

Tilly was on her feet, by this time, heading across the
room.

"I *did* buy a point and a tiny island in Muskoka," she
hurled back at them over her shoulder. "And I was plan-
ning to have the lot of you up to visit me this summer.
Now I'm not so sure I want you. Janie and I have no
trouble believing in each other. I wouldn't want you
doubting my word every time I turned around."

"Till, don't be ridiculous," Mother finally managed to
stem the flood of words.

She and Dad were in the hall now, with Tilly. Rob,
Elaine and Janie sat where they were. None of them
looked at each other.

"Heavens, Matilda, what an outburst," Dad said. He
sounded embarrassed.

Then, Janie was stunned to hear her mother say slowly
and painfully, "I . . . maybe you're right, Tilly. I see
what you mean, although I didn't notice it before. You
always have understood Janie better than I. Rob and
Elaine . . ."

Dad shut the door. The three children could hear only
a murmur of voices now. They still sat, not one of them
knowing what to do or say.

Janie was dazed. Tilly had gone into battle for her, like a knight riding into a tournament. It had been wonderful, for a moment, but frightening too. Now, as she strained her ears to hear what was being said in the hall, she saw with a flash of insight that Tilly had been only partly right. Mother had told her, Janie, over and over again that nobody trusts a liar. She thought of her own way of weighing everything Lisa said, testing for flaws, looking for what did not fit, ever since she had discovered that Lisa lied. She was Lisa's friend — but she knew better than to believe Lisa without question. She, herself, had made her family distrust her. If she wanted them to take what she said on faith, she would have to stick to what was true until she had earned their trust.

It was a difficult thought. She would not have been able to work it out except that Mother had explained it to her so often. She had not listened — but she had heard.

"Hey, you guys," she said. Her voice seemed to thunder in the silence but she went on bravely. "You wait till you see Tilly's place. There's a marvelous rock you can dive right off and, Rob, Mr. Hollis told us there's terrific fishing."

"We may never get there," Elaine said in a growl.

Then, startling the three of them, came a burst of laughter from the hallway. The three adults were having fun together, not fighting any longer.

"Oh yes, you will," Janie smiled. "You'll see."

9

Steffy Catches On

JANIE gobbled her breakfast with the speed of light on Monday morning. She could scarcely contain herself. Wait till the other girls heard about her own private island. Well, Tilly's island really — but Tilly herself had said that she was getting it for Janie.

She was on the step watching for the others five minutes before they appeared. As they came down the sidewalk, Rob wheeled his bicycle out of the garage. Lisa darted away from Debbie and Pam.

"Hi, Rob," she breathed, popping up right in front of him so that he had to stop for a moment if only to navigate around her.

"Hello," Rob grinned down at her pixy face.

"How about offering a girl a ride on your handlebars?" Lisa suggested.

"One girl I might be able to handle, but four, no

thanks!" Rob answered, turning the wheel and starting around her.

Lisa shifted so that she again blocked his path.

"I don't mean *them,*" she said scornfully, jerking her shoulder at Janie, Debbie and Pam who stood in a row, watching. "They need the exercise. How about taking just me?"

Rob laughed. "Ask me again in five years, Lisa, and you might have yourself a date," he told her.

With a quick move, he maneuvered the bike past her, swung himself onto it and sped away down the road toward the high school.

Lisa simply stood where she was, gazing after him, her eyes shining.

"You'd think she'd catch on that, to him, she's just a little kid," Pam made a low comment.

Janie's eyes widened and both Pam and Debbie laughed. Lisa had still not joined them. Debbie summed it up.

"You'd think Steffy would catch on that, to our Lisa, she's just Rob's kid sister," she taunted.

So that was what Lisa had meant on that first day when she said, "I've been hearing things about you, Jane Chisholm." She must have only lately discovered that Rob and Janie were related. No wonder she was forever asking questions about him, his taste in records, his favorite color. Janie should have felt wounded but she could not. It was too funny. The thought of anyone thinking Rob was something special tickled her and she giggled.

Pam joined her and, belatedly, Debbie.

"What's so funny?" Lisa came quickly to where they waited.

"It's Steffy," Debbie answered. "She's being silly, that's all."

Suddenly, Lisa remembered what Janie had told them about Tilly's mysterious "expedition."

"What did that woman want?" she questioned, as she went ahead, with Pam today. "Did she give you a present or anything?"

Janie spilled out the whole story.

"She sounds crazy," Lisa said when Janie told about the ad in the paper. "Is she rich?"

"Rich? Tilly? Heavens, no! She's an artist. She lectures at the University on art, too, but she's certainly not rich."

Lisa looked disappointed. Janie went on. When she got to the part about the island, she saw a new Pam. The girl who had seemed dull and lackluster to Janie had turned and was walking backwards so that she would not miss a word. Her face was bright with wonder and astonishment, as though she had been with Janie in those few moments on the little island. Janie could not tell them about singing Taps out there. Lisa and Debbie would have laughed at her. But, sometime, when she and Pam were by themselves, she might be able to share it with her.

"You mean to say there's no cottage at all?" Lisa asked.

"None," Janie said happily. "We're going to live in a tent this summer, Tilly says, and she's going to have a little cabin built maybe. Just one room. 'Just enough roof to get in under when it rains,' she said."

"Is there a boat?" Debbie wanted to know.

Janie shook her head.

"A dock?"

"No."

"A raft or diving board?"

"No, of course not. I told you — just land."

"Heavens," Lisa said dryly, "and you sounded all excited! Why, there'd be absolutely nothing to do in a place like that. Is there a town close by?"

"I think Tilly said the nearest one is four or five miles away." Janie tried to be accurate.

Somehow, as they talked, Debbie and Pam had changed places. Debbie and Lisa were clearly in complete agreement over Tilly's property.

"I can't see what you're all steamed up about, Steffy." Debbie made a face. "My parents want to go to our cottage for a month and I'm begging them to let me stay in town with my aunt. There's no TV there, no shows, nobody to talk to but the family, nowhere to go."

"No boys!" Lisa put in, and she and Debbie laughed.

Janie thought of the Point — of all the picnic places, of

the swimming she would do, of the rocks where she could curl up with her book, of the woods to explore.

She tried to keep her face blank so that Lisa and Debbie would not see there how she pitied them.

"Oh, Janie, you're so lucky," Pam murmured.

Janie nodded. "I know," she said simply.

10

At Lisa's

ALL WEEK, Janie waited for Lisa to mention the fact that she had invited Janie to spend the night at her house on Friday. Lisa had suggested Monday first, but Mother had refused to let Janie go visiting on a school night. The days passed. Lisa did not refer to it.

Janie tried to bring herself to say, "I'm looking forward to Friday night." She would get the words ready. She would have them right on the tip of her tongue. But, somehow or other, they were never spoken.

Debbie and Pam were always with the other two. Perhaps that was why Lisa did not say anything. Perhaps she was being tactful. Janie, knowing Lisa better by now, did not honestly think that tact would keep Lisa quiet, although she could not find any other explanation.

When Friday itself arrived, Janie was decidedly uneasy. Suppose Lisa had forgotten! The Chisholms were expect-

ing Janie to go. Dad was going to drive her over after
supper. Mother had even bought her new pajamas to wear,
gay shortie ones with ruffles across the seat.

Finally, in the afternoon as they were going from Art to
Music, Janie did manage to go hurriedly, almost under her
breath, "I'll see you after supper, Lisa."

"Huh?" Lisa responded. Then, an expression Janie
could not fathom crossed her face. "Oh . . . sure, Steffy,"
she said lightly, brushing past and preceding Janie into
the classroom.

Janie did not try again but, inside her, a guard went up.
Whatever happened, she was prepared.

The family made much over her as they helped her
pack. Ever since Tilly's surprising outburst, the Chisholms
had been trying harder to make Janie feel their love and
concern. As Elaine came in to offer her silver-backed comb
and brush set; as Rob called up, "Are you ever lucky to be
visiting Matt Daniels! Let me know if he wants to hear
some teen-age talent, won't you?"; as Mother helped her
pack and Tim thoughtfully unpacked everything Mother
had so carefully arranged in the suitcase, Janie groaned
to herself. They were trying so hard. They were being so
nice. They imagined that they were doing what Tilly
would have done, behaving toward her as David did.
Janie knew, in that moment, Tilly and David would have
seen that she was worried about going to Lisa's. Tilly and
David would have stopped getting ready long enough to

find out what had gone wrong. But the others did love her — and she loved them.

"Thanks a lot, Elaine," she said, handling the comb and brush reverently.

"Okay, I'll get you an audition," she yelled back at Rob.

"That's perfect, Mom," she told her Mother — and then, they both laughed at Tim and his helpful ways.

It seemed only seconds later that she and Dad were pulling up in front of the Fairview Apartment where the Danielses lived.

"Shall I just drop you here, Janie?" Dad asked. "I guess you know your way, don't you."

"No . . . please, wait for me, Daddy." Janie slipped into the childish name without thinking. She added, still not getting out of the car, "I've never been here before."

Then, her father astonished her by saying, just as Tilly would have, "Why don't I walk up with you? I'd like to see inside and we might as well make sure she's really expecting you."

Janie was too grateful for speech. They went together into the lobby. Dad found the right button and pushed it. A voice came through a speaker in the wall.

"Who is it?"

"Jim Chisholm," Dad said, his voice strong and sure.

"Oh . . ." the woman sounded startled. "Okay. I'll buzz for the door to open."

"Heavens," Dad said mildly, as the buzzer sounded,

the door clicked and he and Janie pushed through it into the long, carpeted hall. "What a place for a child!"

Janie was not sure what he meant but she was glad she was not Lisa. It was so hushed, so rich-looking, so dead. Nobody would ever, ever dare to run or sing in a place like this.

The elevator slid them silently to the fourteenth floor. The Daniels' apartment was down the hall to the right. A lady was standing at the door. This was not Lisa's mother, Janie knew. She was much too roundabout and elderly to be a model.

"Yes, Mr. Chisholm, what can I do for you?" she asked pleasantly.

Janie just stood. Dad explained. The lady looked distressed.

"I'm so sorry, darling," she said, peering down at Janie.

Janie winced at the endearment.

"Lisa's gone to the theater with her parents and Debbie . . . Debbie . . ."

"Wellington," Janie supplied automatically.

"I think that *is* the name," the lady agreed. "She must have completely forgotten you were coming for she never once mentioned it. I keep house for Mrs. Daniels and I would have known if Lisa'd been expecting anyone. I see that things are ready. Are you sure you didn't get the dates mixed up, honey? Perhaps it was next weekend . . ."

"But . . ." began Janie. The words stuck in her throat. She looked up at her father.

"I'm sure there's been some such mistake, Mrs. . . ."

"Wallace," the lady supplied.

"Wallace," Dad echoed, his hand cupping around Janie's shoulder and squeezing comfortingly. "Would you mind not mentioning this to Lisa when she comes home? Janie would rather Lisa didn't know she got mixed up about it, wouldn't you, Janie?"

"Yes," Janie said.

Mrs. Wallace assured them she would never say a word. She was going on about the Daniels family when Dad, politely but firmly, withdrew himself and his daughter from the doorway and escaped to the elevator.

All the way down, Janie's heart grew heavier and heavier. She did not mind not staying, but Dad must think she had made up the whole thing, invitation and all.

They were in the car. The car was on its way home. Then Dad spoke.

"That was a cruel thing Lisa did, Janie," he said.

"Lisa did!" Janie's heart leapt.

"But, Dad, you said I'd got it 'mixed up,' " she quoted him.

"Suppose Lisa did forget. I can see you think she did not and I suspect you are right, but let's suppose, for a moment, that she honestly forgot. It would make her feel

badly to learn that you had come and found her not home, wouldn't it?"

"Sure," Janie said, following him, but unconvinced about Lisa's innocence.

"Now, let's suppose, instead, that she did it on purpose. Maybe she didn't mean to, at first, but then, when her parents arranged this theater trip, suppose Lisa deliberately let you think you could still come and spend the night with her. We all have a mean streak, Janie. Maybe Lisa has a bigger one than some, but we all have one. Think how powerful she'd feel when she came home and discovered you'd actually taken her at her word and come — and found she'd gone."

"Oh," Janie said slowly. She was beginning to see.

"Mrs. Wallace has promised not to tell her. I think we can trust her though I would not be surprised if that woman loves to talk. But she *did* promise. Now, Janie, if I were you, I wouldn't say a word."

"Let Lisa wonder, you mean," Janie filled in. "Not say anything at all?"

"Not a word," Dad said solemnly. "If she forgot, it is the kind thing to do. If she didn't forget, it . . ."

"It will serve her right," said Janie. The car had come to a stop. Her father was waiting for her to get out and go on in. They were certainly going to be surprised to see her back so soon, Janie thought. She leaned over her suitcase, bulky on the seat between them, and gave her father a quick, almost shy kiss.

"Thanks, Dad," she said.

"Think nothing of it," Dad grinned at her. "It's all part of being a parent. One gets used to the unexpected. Now, away you go and tell the others."

Relief suddenly rose in Janie like bubbles in new ginger-ale. She bounced out of the car and flew up the walk. She did not have to go to Lisa's. She could sleep in her own bed! And she still had the new pajamas!!!

11

"Your Brother's Home!"

NOBODY but Tim noticed Janie's joyous entrance.

"Janie! Janie!" he yelled and threw himself at her knees.

Janie was not flattered. He went through the same performance every afternoon when each of them came in from school. But she was glad to see him. She scooped him up and hugged him till he squeaked. He was laughing uproariously at her when Mother appeared to see who was making the commotion.

"Janie!" she cried. The delight in her voice was so like Tim's that Janie was startled. She had left only half an hour ago. Mother should have been astonished to see her — but she looked excited instead.

"I'm so glad to see you, though I've no idea why you're here," she said, sounding as scatterbrained as Janie had ever heard her. "Your brother's home."

Janie stared at her. Then the meaning of the words dawned on her.

"David!"

"Yes, he's in the living room. Go on in and . . ."

But Janie did not wait to be told. Dropping Tim, she raced for the living room door. David, hearing her voice, came hurrying to find her. Crash! They collided head-on. Janie gasped for air and went to stand back and give David room to breathe. David, however, was not interested in breathing. He crushed his younger sister in a bear hug, until she squealed for mercy just as Tim had done earlier.

"They told me you were out for the evening," he said, when, at last, he let her go.

"Yes, Janie. Why aren't you at Lisa's?" Elaine said suddenly.

"I think Lisa did a neat double-cross," Dad explained, grinning a welcome at his tall son, even as he started to tell the others about Lisa's not being there.

Janie's eyes searched every face, watching for the "This is one of Janie's stories" look. But nobody was doubting her. They were angry. Even Mother, who was forever reminding them that people "meant well," looked as though she would like to get her hands on Lisa Daniels. Rob spoke up suddenly.

"I wasn't going to tell you because I thought the kid was such a friend of yours, Janie," he said, "but she's an awful pill of a kid, if you ask me. She actually was waiting

for me outside the school the other day when I came out after my exam. There I am, with a whole bunch of guys, and here's this ten-year-old kid yelling 'Rob! Rob!' "

He called his own name in a falsetto imitation of Lisa, and Janie doubled over with laughter. Through her giggles, she did straighten him out though. "She's not ten. She's twelve!"

"Ten . . . twelve, what's the difference! She's still an infant in arms!"

"Expecially when you're all of fifteen yourself!" David teased.

"Aw, cut it out!" Rob growled, aiming a poke at his brother.

"Go on, Rob. What happened?" Elaine begged.

"Well, she kept on like that and the others said, 'Who's your friend, Robert?' and stuff like that. Rocky Jamieson said, 'Aren't you going to speak to the little lady, Rob? We'll chaperone.' Well . . ."

"Stop saying 'well' all the time — but go on," Mother urged, annoyed with herself for interrupting him.

"Well . . . I mean . . . I said, 'What do you want, kid?' I thought maybe Janie needed something. Heck, I didn't know what. But she looks at me all gooey-like and she says, 'I'm late getting home, Rob. Would you mind riding me home on your crossbar?"

"So did you?" Dad said. His eyes twinkled.

"Are you kidding?" Rob yelped. "I just told her the

truth. The whole brutal truth. I said, 'Look, kid, I'm too big to play with little girls. And you don't happen to live out my way. You're ten years too young for me,' I told her, 'and going the way you're going, add ten years on and I still wouldn't be interested.' "

David whistled. Dad shook his head over Rob's gentlemanly behavior. Mother laughed. Elaine applauded. Janie stood very still, feeling suddenly sorry for Lisa.

"So that's why no Lisa was there tonight," Dad said slowly. "She was taking revenge. Janie was the logical one to lash out at. I think, Janie, that you'd better be *sure* not to mention this to Lisa."

"Don't worry," Janie said earnestly. "I wouldn't know what to say. But I wish I didn't have to walk with her on Monday. Maybe, if I called Pam . . ."

"Jim, I think now might be the time," Mother said.

"Time for what?" Dad looked at her blankly.

Janie, still worrying about Monday morning, was not paying much attention. Calling Pam would not solve things. She would just have to explain. She was almost sure Pam would understand. But Pam might tell. And even if she did not, she and Janie would still have to walk with Lisa and Debbie, as always, or Lisa *would* know her revenge had worked.

"Oh, Jim, really!" sighed Mother. "Remember what brought David here tonight."

Why had David come? Janie began to listen. David had

a job working in Riverside, this summer, for Andrew Copeland. He was doing construction work and getting hard muscles and a deep, deep tan doing it. But he had not been coming home for weekends. It was too far to come and, besides, he was dating Sally Copeland.

"Oh . . . of course," Dad said. "I'd forgotten just for the minute. Rob's gallant way with women put it out of my head."

Rob blushed and they all laughed.

"But I agree," Dad said then. "No time like the present. A pun, Mary! No time like the 'present' . . ."

"Really!" Mother said again, disgusted with him. She had no patience with his puns. All the children were punsters too. And, according to Mother, she had yet to hear any of them, children or father, make one really good one.

Now she turned to Janie who was on the verge of asking what on earth they were talking about.

"Janie," she said, smiling a special smile that made Janie's heart begin to thump. Something was about to happen. "You *do* remember what is going to happen here on July seventeenth, don't you?"

"My birthday," Janie replied, her eyes popping.

"Well," Mother began.

Rob could not resist. "I do wish you wouldn't say 'well' all the time, Mother," he scolded her.

"What?" she said, startled, stopping what she was saying. Janie wanted to shriek. She controlled herself with iron will power.

"Mother!" she begged.

"Don't you interrupt me again, Robert, whatever I say!" Mother commanded. "Oh Janie, I'm sorry. Well . . . I mean, David has brought your present, from your father and me, here from Riverside. It's secondhand. He found out they wanted to sell it and asked for it. Meg Copeland's too big for it now, but I'm sure it will be just right for you. And your father agreed. So, instead of waiting till your birthday . . ."

"Mary, for goodness sake, her birthday is going to come and go while you stand and talk." Dad halted the flood of words. "Go on out and bring it in, David."

David, who had been waiting too, dashed out to the garage. Elaine was jigging up and down by now, not at all like a sedate fourteen-year-old.

"Oh, Janie, just wait till you see!" she sang at her sister.

"David gone?" Tim said in a worried voice.

"He's coming back, darling," Mother told him, but she never took her eyes off Janie's face. Thus, she caught the blaze of glory there when David struggled through the doorway and placed, squarely in front of his sister, the bicycle of her dreams.

Janie stared at it, her mouth agape, looked around at the beaming circle of faces, tried to speak, made a croaking noise instead, and then, grabbed Tim to her and hugged him all over again. He was not too surprised. He was used to being loved by his family.

"Janie, Janie," he said tenderly, patting her cheek with his pudgy hand.

And Janie promptly, wetly and happily, burst into tears.

12

Pam

JANIE heard the kitchen clock strike one that night.
She was too happy, too strung up with excitement,
to sleep. She lay awake, not minding a bit, and dreamed
of riding her bicycle. She pictured Meg Copeland riding
it. David had told them about Meg. She had ginger hair
like Janie's own and she was a family rebel, too, except
that she was the baby of her family. She was in high
school now and was becoming quite a tennis player, according to David. Her bike had not been used in the last
couple of years. High school girls, in Riverside, did not
ride bicycles.

"They must be crazy," Janie told herself. But she
thought gratefully of Meg, all the same. Dad knew Mr.
Copeland. They had gone to school together. And David
talked of the family as though he had been friends with

them for years rather than just a few weeks. Maybe, some-day, Janie would meet Meg.

Her thoughts left Meg and returned to the bicycle. It had been painted and repaired. It had a brand-new bell, David's present, and a basket hung on its handlebars. Meg had used that. Janie imagined herself riding, winging free and wild as the wind, swooping up one street and down another, her hair blowing back, her cheeks cooled by the breeze she herself was making.

It could not possibly be as wonderful as her imagina-tion made it. Yet, when she actually climbed onto the bike and sailed away down the street, she discovered that it was better. The real thing was so much more . . . real. She sped along, pedaling furiously, coasting down hills, getting off and pushing up them a couple of times. And it was so perfect that she could scarcely believe it.

All weekend, she rode her bicycle. Sunday School stopped her for an hour, church for another. But she did not waste time arguing. She was using every last minute to ride and then looking forward to the moment when she would be free to ride again.

"I'll forget what you look like," Mother warned her.

Janie only laughed.

Lisa was not at Sunday School. Janie had wondered if she might be and had readied herself to face her there. She was relieved when Lisa did not show up. Miss Andrews noticed a difference in Janie the moment she saw her.

"What's happened to set you aglow?" she asked.

"I have a new bicycle," Janie told her.

"Oh, Janie, how lovely. I know how you've longed for one. Is it everything you dreamed it would be?" Miss Andrews asked, smiling.

Janie nodded. "Everything," she said.

She almost forgot to telephone Lisa to tell her not to call for her in the morning. She remembered as she came into the house after racing around the park three times on the bike.

"Hello," Lisa answered the phone herself.

"Hi, Lisa," Janie panted into her ear. "This is me, Janie."

"Janie," Lisa's voice sharpened. Then she drawled slowly, "What's the matter?"

"Nothing, nothing at all," Janie told her gaily. "I just called to tell you not to bother picking me up tomorrow. I have a new bike. I'll be riding to school from now on."

"A what?" Lisa could not believe her ears.

"A bicycle," Janie said plainly. " 'Bye, Lisa."

"My mother says they're dangerous!" Lisa shrilled before Janie could hang up.

"My mother doesn't," Janie said sweetly.

Click. The receiver was back in place. She had done it.

Janie reached school first on Monday. With nearly half an hour to spare, she got involved with the people in a book. When Lisa, Debbie and Pam came in, carried along on a wave of Lisa's bright chatter, Janie did not even notice them for a moment. Portia and Julian, in Elizabeth Enright's *Gone-away Lake,* were taking her whole attention.

Lisa would have ignored her in return. Perhaps, even if Janie had spoken, Lisa would have passed her by. Neither of them was quite sure what she should do. But Pam had other ideas.

"Janie, have you really, truly got a bike?" she demanded.

"Yup!" Janie said, laconically. Her eyes were gleaming with pride, though. Pam was not fooled.

"Oh, everything nice happens to you!" she said.

Janie had been happy clear through, but Pam's words came as a shock. She had known she was lucky. She was delighted with her bike. But she had been a misfit for so long that she was used to feeling slightly sorry for herself. Pam's eyes, dark with envy, left no room inside Janie for self-pity.

"Nice things happen to you too," she said lamely.

"Name one," Pam countered.

"Pam, that was the bell," Lisa hissed. Pam scuttled to her desk. It was time to begin being enriched.

Janie only half-liked "enrichment" days. She and her

friends were all in the "bright" class. Very few of them had any examinations to write. Instead, they saw films, heard speakers, went on field trips. But always, in the back of Janie's mind, were the other boys and girls in the school. She could feel them, see them almost, scowling anxiously at the examination questions, chewing the ends of pencils, wondering whether or not they would pass. Elaine had been such a student. She still had to work very hard and get extra help to make average grades. Janie had often heard her bitter comments on "the smart kids" and their "smugness." Janie never had a defense ready when Elaine began. She knew that many of her classmates *were* smug. She knew that she, herself, would never think of telling the rest her guilty feelings about being "enriched."

"Who needs to be enriched the most?" Elaine would ask.

Her argument made sense to Janie. Maybe, if Elaine had been allowed to see films like this one, she would have become excited about Math. Maybe. Janie shook her mind free and tried to get excited herself.

They had recess that day. Now that they were in junior high, recess was usually a thing of the past. Janie felt like a little girl again as the class swarmed out onto the playground. The others must have shared her feelings this time, for in less than a minute some were playing tag, some hopscotch on the squares painted for the Primary

children, and one giggling group was circling around playing London Bridge.

Janie was content to watch. It was hot. The sky was
as blue as a sky could be. It made her eyes ache to look up
at it for more than an instant. She leaned against the wall,
luxuriating in just plain dreaming of nothing in particular. Pam joined her quietly, leaned with her, perhaps even
dreamed the same dream.

"You two look like a couple of cows," Lisa said fretfully,
breaking out of the lineup for London Bridge and coming
over to stand in front of them. Janie blinked lazily at her.
It was a good description. Right at that moment, she felt
as contented, as placid as a cow.

"Nice cows," she said drowsily. "Aren't we, Pam?"

Pam laughed deep in her throat. She sounded as
though she were laughing in her sleep.

"Oh, honestly," Lisa stamped her foot at them. "Where's
the new bicycle?"

Janie came awake at that. Her eyelids, heavy with sunshine and laziness, flew up. She smiled broadly at Lisa,
her friend after all.

"Over in the bike stand. Come on and I'll show you,"
she offered, shoving herself out from the wall and starting
off.

Lisa smiled, a small satisfied smile.

"No, thanks, Stuffy," she said clearly. "I've seen plenty
of bikes before. I'm sure yours is nothing special. I just

wanted to know if you really had one or were only telling one of your usual lies."

She turned on her heel, leaving Janie staring after her. Over her shoulder, she tossed back, "Coming, Pam?"

"Not right now," Pam answered.

"Suit yourself," Lisa said, her back still turned. Then she was back in the game, playing as noisily as anyone there, paying no attention to the two by the wall.

"She wanted you to say that," Pam commented.

"I know," Janie said dully.

The morning no longer seemed to shine. There was something hurtful about the way Lisa had walked away. Janie tried to put it out of her mind. She had finished with Lisa already. Lisa was not her friend, had not been her friend ever, really. Lisa had wanted Rob to notice her, that was all. Janie reminded herself of these facts. There was no arguing with any of them. Lisa had lied to her. Lisa had hurt her on purpose. Lisa had a mean streak, all right, as Dad had said — except Lisa's mean streak ran right through her.

"She feels bad," Pam said slowly, her thoughts following Janie's.

"I know," Janie said again. She did not know how she knew. She was not even sure she and Pam were right. But there had been a lost look to Lisa's shoulders as she walked away from them, a hunched-up look, as though she felt alone now that they had deserted her.

"Only *she's* the one who did it to herself," Janie protested, through Pam had not spoken in Lisa's defense.

This time it was Pam who said, "I know."

They leaned again, not really contented this time, just two girls waiting for the bell to call them back to class.

"Tell me about your point and island again," asked Pam, after a couple of moments of silence.

Happiness flowed back into Janie like a golden river. Words spilled out of her. This time, softly so that no one else would catch a word of it, she did tell Pam about her first trip out to the tiny island, about singing Taps to it, about the silence there and the stars. "And in just two weeks, Tilly and I will be there!" she finished exultantly.

Pam's sigh brought her back to earth.

"What do you do in the summers, Pam?" she asked, more out of politeness than curiosity.

"I stay right here most of the time," Pam said dully. "My aunt gets only a two-week holiday and she takes it in the fall. She goes out West to visit my other aunt and I stay with my grandmother then. We go for drives on weekends sometimes, but my aunt doesn't like cottages. She says it's more comfortable right at home. I guess, for her, it is. She has arthritis and . . . well, anyway, that's what I do."

Janie remembered now. Pam's parents had been killed when the bus they were riding on had collided with a train. It had happened years before, when Pam was only two or three. Pam's aunt worked in a dry goods store down-town. Before that, it seemed to Janie, she had worked for Lisa's mother. She had had something to do with Lisa's mother anyway. Someone had guessed once that Lisa put up with Pam because their families were friends . . . or something. It was vague in Janie's mind. When she had heard it, she had not known she and Pam would ever be friends.

"Friends," she thought wonderingly. "I suppose we are. Not Lisa and me . . . Pam and me."

"I'm sorry, Pam," she said uncertainly.

"It's okay. I'm used to it," Pam told her.

The bell rang. As the boys and girls streamed back into the school, Pam hurried to catch up with Lisa.

13

Blue Lake and Rocky Shore

S CHOOL was over, Tilly had come to stay and tomorrow she and Janie were leaving for Muskoka.
The little car was ready to carry a mountain of belong-
ings. It had a roof-top carrier fixed on top and a trailer,
which Tilly had borrowed, hitched on behind.

"And I *still* don't see how you're ever going to get it
all in," Mother said, gazing at the equipment piling up
in the hall.

Janie had been having the time of her life. She and
Tilly had been on a shopping binge. Nobody Janie had
ever shopped with spent money in the lavish, unexpected,
quixotic way Tilly did. The Chisholms, managing on a
bank manager's salary, had to count the cost of everything
and plan and save before they could afford any major

purchase. Janie would have had her bicycle a couple of years earlier if David had not had college expenses, if Elaine had not had to have her teeth straightened, if Tim had not had to go to the doctor about his allergies, if Dad had not bought a new used car, if the washing machine had not broken down . . . But Tilly had only herself and Janie to worry about. She said she would be paying for the Point for years, but she intended to have a few other things along the way.

Janie followed along, wide-eyed with delight, as they bought sleeping bags, air mattresses, a camp stove and fuel for it, a Coleman lantern, an animal-proof cooler, a tent, a big flashlight, mosquito lotion and spray, jackets with hoods for both of them, rubber boots for Tilly (Janie had a pair). Then Tilly bought an oven! Janie gaped.

"You mean we're going to bake without electricity!" she said.

"Sure," Tilly answered recklessly. "We can do just about anything. Now, what we need next is a closet."

"A closet!" squeaked Janie.

Tilly prowled along the aisle of the department store, looking for a closet. She explained that they would not have room to store much in their tent. If they could just find a closet, a waterproof closet, that would hang in a tree . . .

"Tilly, there's no such thing!"

"That's what you think," jeered Tilly.

And she found her closet. It was really a plastic container which you were supposed to hang up inside your closet in the house, zippered up the front, with shelves for hats.

"Just what we need," said Tilly, and bought it.

The car groaned under the weight of everything they had bought and collected from here and there. Tilly even had a pile of boards in the back and twenty bricks. Janie could not imagine what she planned to build with them.

"Wait and see," was all the satisfaction she got.

They drove and drove. It took nearly three hours. Janie slept part of the way. But when they got into the northern country of rocks and blue lakes, she sat watching every inch of the road, looking for landmarks. Everything looked familiar and yet nothing was quite right until, all at once, they came over the brink of a hill, the car stopped suddenly and then began to inch slowly downward and Janie cried,

"Tilly, it's your hill!! We're there!!!"

"Don't distract me," Tilly said between her teeth. "We're not there until I land this trailer safely."

Moments later, they pulled up where they had parked before and there it was — tall trees, sky, blue lake, even the sunset, all waiting for Janie.

"Now we eat!" Janie said happily, remembering the

food they had bought, her favorite things — hot dogs, eggs, bacon, chocolate cake . . .

"Now we put up the tent," Tilly corrected her. "If we can," she added.

Janie had had no idea how complicated one tent could be. Tilly had been given instructions, but she had to keep stopping to consult them while Janie stood holding up a side and hoping she was doing the right thing. The mosquitoes whirred around her, nipping at her neck and the backs of her knees. She had no hand free to slap them. It was sheer anguish, but not for one moment did she wish she and Tilly had not come.

At last, it was up. The sun had gone down while they worked but it was still twilight. The bugs were at their worst.

"Cannibals!" Tilly said, swatting two at once.

The tent leaned a little but it was a house just the same. Janie ducked her head and went inside. She sat on the grass and looked out through the open flap. There lay the still lake. Three stars shone in the evening sky. Janie swallowed. It was so beautiful she had a lump in her throat just looking.

"Jane Chisholm, get out here and get to work," Tilly ordered.

They carted the sleeping bags in. Then Tilly brought in her bricks and boards. To Janie's amazement, she built a bookcase right there in the tent. The ground was not quite even but, with a flat stone to help her, Tilly soon had her shelves erected.

Janie was enough her mother's daughter to be taken aback. With all they still had to do, it seemed crazy for Tilly to be putting up bookshelves. Tilly caught the look on her face and laughed at her.

"Listen to me, Stephanie Jane," she said, and there was a serious note under the laughter which Janie did not miss. "I would not live in a place, not even in a tent on my own point, without a place for books. I brought some for both of us. The shelves can hold other things too. Just make sure they don't touch the walls and let the rain in. Here, you can arrange these."

Janie carried in a box of Kleenex, a jar of cold cream, two decks of cards, the flashlight, and three armfuls of books. It was almost too dark to see the titles, but she did make out Eleanor Estes' *The Moffats*, Rosemary Sutcliff's *Warrior Scarlet*, Mary Stolz's *The Noon Day Friends*, Mabel Robinson's *Bright Island*, Frances Hodgson Burnett's *A Little Princess*, Rumer Godden's *Miss Happiness and Miss Flower*, T. S. Eliot's *Book of Practical Cats*, and *The Oxford Book of Poetry for Children*. There were others she did not know. She hugged herself, anticipating the fun before her.

When the car was half unpacked ("Enough for one

night!" Tilly groaned) the two of them crawled into the tent and ate cookies and oranges.

"That was a funny supper," Janie said, "and my hands are sticky."

"Let's go swimming and clean them." Tilly jumped up and began to get ready. Janie gasped and then hurried to catch up.

"You're not supposed to swim right after you eat and you're not supposed to go in in the dark," she scolded, as she skinned out of her clothes.

"Yes, Grandma, I know," Tilly teased. She went on more seriously, "You are right, Janie, but we won't really swim. And it isn't quite dark yet. We'll just go down and paddle in Tim's Cove."

Janie said, "That's okay then."

But secretly, she was a bit disappointed to find out that Tilly was sensible after all.

They splashed each other and shrieked. The water was cold even though it had been a sunny day. There had been a brisk wind and only the surface had been warmed.

"It's a good thing we're the only people up here," Tilly gasped, as she ducked a flying fistful of water Janie aimed at her. "We'd be having a rescue squad out with the noise we're making."

When the two of them got dry, they climbed into their pajamas and curled deep down in the warmth of their sleeping bags.

"This is positively the earliest I've gone to bed in years," Tilly yawned. "But I'm exhausted."

She peered at her watch, luminous in the dark.

"It's not even nine o'clock," she exclaimed.

Janie snuggled deeper into her sleeping bag. She would not go to bed till the last minute, at home, but it was different here. Now, through the tent flap, she could see dozens of stars spangling the reaches of the sky.

"What are Lisa and Company doing this summer?" Tilly inquired.

"Lisa's going to Europe," Janie said, without a trace of envy in her voice. "She talked about it all the time at the end of school. Her Dad is going on a business trip or something. Maybe it's Mrs. Daniels. I don't know. Anyway, they'll be away all summer. They're going to Spain and Italy and I forget where else."

"And . . . Debbie, is it?" Tilly wanted to know.

Janie grinned in the dark.

"She's gone to her cottage with her family. She told everybody she'd kill herself before she'd go — but she went. I saw them go by. Poor Debbie."

"What is the other girl's name?" Tillie probed.

"Pam Potter," Janie said slowly, her laughter dying away. "Pam's just staying home with her aunt."

She told Tilly about Pam. Tilly listened quietly and completely, the way Tilly always listened. Janie found herself going on to tell of how she and Pam were nearly friends.

"Not like Lisa . . . real friends. Maybe, anyway," Janie finished. "I wish Pam had a Tilly," she added wistfully, after a moment.

"Thank you, Stephanie Jane," said Tilly softly.

14

Dishes and Giant Steps

J ANIE! Lunchtime!" Tilly called.

Janie opened her eyes and blinked at the sunlight. She had dozed off again, lying there on the warm bright rocks, with her book open before her. It was such a good book too, but on the island, there was never any hurry. Nobody was going to interrupt her. She had forever to saunter through the story.

"Jan-ie!" Tilly yelled.

Janie scrambled up. The book slid away from her, down the slanting rock. Janie dove for it and caught it before it slipped into the water. Someone was interrupting her after all. Not that she minded. She was as hungry as a hunter.

"Coming, Silly Tilly," she called back — and holding the book high in the air, so that it wouldn't get splashed, she waded back to the mainland.

Tilly had baked raspberry cobbler in her Coleman oven. She rushed Janie through her cheese sandwich so that they could taste her creation. Down the Point from them, men had come to start work on Tilly's "mansion." Janie took each of them a serving of the dessert. They smacked their lips appreciatively.

"Your aunt's a good cook," Mr. Whitman said, scraping the last crumb out of the bottom of the dish.

"She's not my aunt, but I'll tell her," Janie promised.

There was half a floor there now. Janie took a big jump and landed on it.

"I hope you're going to build a step," she said, getting her balance.

"Anything you say, Janie," Mr. Whitman agreed, with a lordly wave of his hand.

Janie stood and looked out through an imaginary window. Tilly had chosen a perfect site. The lake shone before her. Of course, it would be hard to find a place on the Point which was not beautiful, Janie reminded herself.

She hopped down, gathered the dishes and returned to Tilly.

"How's the book?" Tilly asked as they washed the dishes.

"Really good," Janie replied. Then, remembering herself falling asleep in the middle of a chapter, she looked a bit abashed. Tilly did not seem to notice.

"Janie," she said suddenly, "we've been here over a week. Are you getting bored?"

"Bored?" Janie stared at her godmother. "Me — bored? Of course not! I love it here!"

"I think you really do," Tilly said, half to herself. Then, as though she were answering some question only she had heard, she added, "But I know it must get pretty lonely for you sometimes. Well, your birthday is only two days away now. I have a plan."

Janie said nothing. She was sure she already guessed what Tilly's plan was. Tilly had to go back to Toronto "to fetch it," she told Janie. And Janie was not to come with her. It was to be a surprise.

Janie was as sure as she could be that Tilly was going to get the rest of the family and bring them up for a party. Janie had never been away from home on her birthday before. She had felt queer thinking about it, until she had figured out what Tilly was scheming. She was leaving Janie at the Hollis' farm for the day. Part of Janie wished she could go along. Part of her was glad she did not have to make the long drive. It would take most of the day going down and then coming back. She had wondered why the Chisholms did not just come up in their own car. Tilly's little bug would never hold them all. Then it came to her that Dad probably had to work. Mother had never learned to drive. Perhaps Dad and Tilly would trade cars for a couple of days.

"I hope I'm guessing right," Tilly said now. "There, that's the last. You can dump the water."

"I'll be practically grown-up on my birthday, Tilly," Janie said, coming back with the dish pan.

"You *look* grown-up, I must say," Tilly snorted.

Janie looked at herself through Tilly's eyes. She was brown as an Indian. She had on a skimpy sky-blue bathing suit. She was barefoot. Before she had come north, she had had her hair cut almost as short as a boy's. "Shorter than some!" Mother had said.

But lots of grown women wore bathing suits and went barefoot and wore their hair short. What was it about her that made Tilly laugh at her? Tilly saw her expression and laughed some more.

"Oh, it's not your clothes or your hair, Janie," she said. "It's not even your figure, though you don't have much of one yet, to say the least. It's just you. You look as round-cheeked and big-eyed and freckle-faced as Tim. But I admit you are growing up, bit by bit."

"I am," Janie said, fascinated with this talk about herself.

"Growing up is like playing a game of 'May I,' " Tilly said. She spoke slowly now, thinking aloud. She was serious. As she talked, the two of them wandered down to the big rock and sat down within comfortable talking distance of each other.

"A game of 'May I!' " Janie was puzzled.

"Well, you take a giant step one day and then, for ages and ages, you just manage baby steps. Once in a while, you even go backward. Then, all at once — and it doesn't happen on a person's birthday necessarily, or even mostly! — you take eight giant steps in a row. Or one of those twirling ones . . . what do you call them?"

"Umbrella steps," Janie informed her. "How about banana steps?"

"They sound slippery," Tilly grinned. "I've taken a few of those. It's a game we all play, you know, Janie. I think I took a giant step the day I bought the Point and became a responsible property owner, all in a minute. I feel quite different."

"You do!" Janie said, frankly astonished. Tilly was Tilly, to her, and always would be. She was a sure thing like the sun in the morning and the stars at night, like the warmth of fire, like the steadiness of earth under your feet.

"Heavens, Stephanie Jane, you make me feel as ancient as Methuselah!" Tilly objected. "I'm still a young thing, comparatively. I've still got years ahead of me to be frivolous in."

"Is that 'growing up?' " asked Janie, her eyes sparkling.

"You stop it! Go away and read your book. I always did think you were an obnoxious child anyway," Tilly said huffily.

Janie laughed and sprawled more comfortably on the rock. Two more days, just two more days till her birthday!

15

A Surprise and a Half

MRS. HOLLIS found her standing at the front window for the sixth time that day.

"Goodness, Jane, you'll wear yourself out watching for them," she teased.

"Well, they could be here by now if they'd hurried," Janie said scanning the empty road.

"Come on out and have some lemonade. I made it specially." Mrs. Hollis was kind. Janie followed her to the kitchen.

Now she was listening. She wished Mrs. Hollis would not be quite so nice. If she would stop talking cheerfully and simply sit and drink her lemonade in silence, Janie might hear the sound of a car turning up the long drive.

It was another hour, though, before they arrived. Janie was back at the window staring at the road with glassy

eyes. She was so tired that the car was one-third of the way up the Hollises' lane before she recognized it. It was not Tilly's car at all. It was Dad's.

Janie tore through the house, burst out the door, and flung herself bodily at her family. She had never dreamed she could be so glad to see them. Until they were there, in front of her, she had not had any idea how much she had missed them, even Elaine. Even Rob!

Then Rob grabbed her, upended her over his knee and started delivering her birthday spanking. Janie yelled for help but only Tim tried gallantly to intervene, clutching Rob around one knee and struggling to rescue his sister. When Rob let her go and shook himself free of Tim, Mother moved in and gave her a kiss and a bone-breaking hug.

"And one to grow on!" she said, adding a little pat on the spot where Rob's far from gentle smack had landed.

"She *has* grown, too," Dad commented, looking his daughter over. "She looks taller — and older, doesn't she, Mary?"

Janie did feel older, more sure of herself, more content to be just Janie. But she was not ready to have that discovered by others yet.

"Where's Tilly?" she asked, creating a diversion.

"She'll be along," Mother told her. "She called us this morning and told us where we'd find you."

"You mean . . . *you* aren't the 'surprise?' " Janie said blankly.

"Well, you certainly looked surprised," Dad said. "You didn't think we'd miss your birthday, did you? We aren't part of whatever Matilda is up to, if that's what you mean. Janie, how about taking us to this Point we've heard so much about?"

"Oh, yes!" cried Janie, remembering with delight that none of the family had yet visited the Point. "Come on. 'Bye, Mrs. Hollis. Thanks a lot."

Mrs. Hollis waved. Jim Chisholm turned the car around. Janie took Tim onto her lap.

"Turn left here, Dad," she said importantly, as they reached the end of the lane.

Dad turned obediently. Tim bounced up and down on Janie's knees. She hugged him close. Oh, she was so glad they were here, so pleased to see each of them. . . . But what was Tilly up to?

The Chisholms reached the bottom of the steep hill safely and turned onto the last little stretch of roadway leading to the Point. Elaine was the first to see it.

"Look," she said, pointing. "They've put up a sign."

"We just put it up yesterday," Janie told them.

"Gilead," Mother read. "Where did Tilly get that? Isn't that some place in the Bible?"

"We sing about 'Gilead' in the choir," Elaine remembered. She sang softly,

"There is a balm in Gilead
To make the wounded whole.
There is a balm in Gilead
To heal the sin-sick soul.

"Sometimes I feel discouraged
And think my work's in vain,
But then, the holy spirit
Revives my soul again.

"There is a balm in Gilead . . ."

"That's it," Janie assured her. "Tilly says that this place is like Gilead because there is a balm here too. And Gilead is just the other side of the Jordan River. Tilly says that when you cross the Jordan, you are supposed to reach Heaven — and her point is heaven on earth, so Gilead is its name."

"That sounds like Tilly," Mother said, getting out of the car.

The family trooped over the Point, exploring every nook and cranny. Elaine and Rob splashed over to the island — and Janie did not mind. She had thought she might but it was fun sharing it with them, and in the bright sunlight, it seemed more of a family place — not the special spot, all her own, that it became early in the morning and around sundown.

Suppertime came — and still no Tilly. Mother produced a barbecued chicken, tomatoes, all things Janie
loved. And to top it, she even had brought a birthday
cake, complete with the seven-minute icing which Janie
always demanded. It had candles on top and favors inside.
For one dreadful minute, Dad pretended to have forgotten
the matches, and then, just as Janie remembered the box-
ful she and Tilly kept, he produced them.

"Happy birthday to you," the Chisholms sang.

Janie held her breath and tried to think of a wish. She
had always wished for a bicycle before, but now, she had
her bike. She had this holiday. She had all she could ask
for . . . except a friend to share it with.

"A friend," she said to herself and blew hard.

Poof! Every flame went out.

"Wait for us," someone called.

Tilly! The family had been so busy concentrating on
Janie and her cake that they had not even heard the car.
They jumped to their feet and started up the hill to meet
her.

Suddenly, Janie stopped. Tilly was not alone. Getting
out of the car, standing uncertainly in the half-light was
a girl. Pam!!!

So that was Tilly's surprise! Janie broke into a run.

Amazing, astonishing, wonderful Tilly!

Then, as she neared the car, she saw the third figure
climb out.

She halted again, jerked to a stop, unable to believe her eyes.

"Hi, Steffy," said Lisa.

16

Pam Explains

JANIE opened her mouth but no sound came out. Lisa was supposed to be in Spain! Lisa was not her friend anyway. Surely Tilly, who understood her better than anyone, knew that much.

Tilly was talking now, covering up the silence with a big hearty voice unlike her own.

"I enjoyed having one girl here with me, so I thought I should have a couple more," she said. "Am I glad you're still here, Jim! I have another tent to put up and Janie and I are not what you'd call skillful at making the things stand erect. I don't suppose you people decided you could stay yourselves, did you?"

"No, we can't," Mother shook her head. "We would have been gone before this except we were waiting for you, of course. Rob goes to camp in the morning and

Elaine is off to visit Camilla Marriott the next day. I could leave you Tim — but not really. I'd die of lonesomeness without him. Besides, you'd probably get reading a book and let him drown!"

"I would *not!*" Tilly protested.

"Hey, a chipmunk is eating the cake!" Rob shouted suddenly, plunging back down the hill.

Awkwardness was forgotten as they hurried after him. The chipmunk had been only about to begin to eat when Rob spotted him, so they were in time. Janie cut the cake, unevenly to be sure, but everyone got a piece. Dad and Tilly gobbled theirs down and went to get the tent. It was growing dark fast. Pam and Lisa were still only speaking when they were spoken to. They were so polite they made Janie more nervous than she already was.

She even wondered, for one hopeful instant, if she might ask Mother and Dad to take her home with them when they left. Then she knew she could not. Tilly must have had some reason . . . and Pam was Janie's friend.

The tent was up. Janie was hugged. She thanked them again for coming and for her bicycle which was, even though she'd been given it early, her birthday present. Elaine had brought her a book and Rob a new shirt which Mother must have chosen. It was a screaming orange and Janie loved it. Tim had solemnly presented her with a tiny stuffed bear he himself had picked out for her. His eyes were so longing that she asked him to keep it for her.

"What a tactful sister!" Dad exclaimed as Tim crooned over the bear, now his to all intents and purposes.

Then, they were gone. Silence threatened again but Tilly was having no part of it. She got the three girls organized.

"Lisa, you can come in with me," she said firmly. "Janie, you and Pam can share the new tent. Maybe Lisa will sleep in and not waken me at dawn!"

Janie was torn. Lisa taking her place with Tilly! But then, she and Pam were going to be together. Maybe, when they went to bed, she would find out what it was all about.

"I adore sleeping in," Lisa said in her drawly voice.

Janie made a rude face at her back. Pam reached out and touched Janie's arm.

"Don't," she said, so softly only Janie could hear. "Wait till I tell you. Miss Barry's wonderful."

Miss Barry . . . That was Tilly. Janie looked doubtful.

"Okay," she muttered to Pam, "but it had better be good."

"It is," Pam said simply.

"What did you say?" Lisa asked, turning.

"I said 'It's good,' " Pam answered. "Good to be here. I love it already."

"Yeah," Lisa answered, her voice shaking a little. "It's

spooky, if you ask me. But I guess it's good too . . . if you like places like this."

Janie could not stand it. What a finish to her birthday.

"Good night," she barked, not looking at anyone in particular. Then she crawled into the tent she was to share with Pam, pulled on her pajamas, determined not to wash her face or brush her teeth, and just lay in her sleeping bag, waiting for Pam to join her or for sleep, whichever came first.

She had not yet calmed down when Pam crawled into the tent.

"Happy Birthday," Pam said.

Happy Birthday! Janie could not say a word. It seemed to her that her birthday had crashed around her. It had been perfect. Tilly had made it so special — and then, there was Lisa. Lisa would hate it at the Point. She had made that clear long before.

"I'd be bored to death in a place like that," Janie remembered her saying.

"Janie," Pam said despairingly, "you're beginning to make me wish I'd never come — and I've been waiting, counting the hours even, ever since Miss Barry's letter."

Janie sat up abruptly. "What letter?" she said. She added, before Pam could answer, "I am glad you came, Pam. I just feel all mixed up. I thought Lisa went to Europe."

"They never ever said they'd take her," Pam said, keeping her voice down. "I think she knew all along they weren't going to. My aunt says that Mrs. Daniels told *her* over a month ago and asked her to keep Lisa for them because their housekeeper was going to take her holiday while they were away. My aunt feels sure they told Lisa then. She says they just decided it all the last minute because her dad realized he wouldn't have any time free to take her around and it would be dangerous for her. She says her mother was worried about her adjusting to the climate too. Every time she talks about it, she tells it a bit differently. But I guess she knows the truth all right. They just plain didn't want to be bothered with her. My aunt says she doesn't blame them."

"I thought they couldn't bear to be without her for even a minute hardly," Janie said slowly, trying to take in this new picture of Lisa.

"Maybe she wishes it were like that." Pam sounded wise. "But Aunt Grace used to work for Mrs. Daniels, you know, before she got arthritis. She used to do typing and stuff. Anyway, she says Mrs. Daniels is so busy it's a wonder she knows she has a daughter. She mostly sees Lisa when she takes her to audition for something and even then, lots of times the housekeeper goes along instead. Her father's really nice. I've met him. I think Lisa gets her niceness from him. But he works all night on that show of his and he sleeps most of the day so she doesn't see much of him either. My Aunt Grace says that

Mr. and Mrs. Daniels don't even see each other. That's mainly why they're going on this trip together."

"So Lisa came to stay with you. I'll bet she hated that," Janie said appreciatively.

"She sure did!" Pam agreed with a sigh. "And so did I! But, I kept thinking, it wouldn't be so bad, because Miss Barry's letter came before Lisa did and she invited me up here for a month. I was so excited I couldn't keep quiet about it. Lisa pretended she didn't care one bit. She said awful things about how dull it was going to be up here and how glad she was she wasn't coming. You couldn't make her come even if you dragged her, she said."

"But she's here!" Janie could not follow the chain of events.

"That's what made us late," Pam said.

Janie was getting impatient now. "Late . . . what do you mean?"

"Well, last night, she came into my room. She woke me up — and Janie, Lisa was crying!"

"Lisa!" Janie did not believe it, except Pam sounded so sure.

"Of course, she can act," Pam admitted, paying Lisa a compliment without intending to. "But this was real, I think. She said she could not bear it if I went away and she had to stay there by herself with Aunt Grace. She begged me to ask Miss Barry if she could, please, come too."

"I thought 'wild horses couldn't drag her' . . ." Janie quoted.

"That's what I said. I told her she'd hate it and I wouldn't. But she said she'd never said any such thing, and if she had, it was just because she was jealous, and she kept on and on . . . and I thought of what it's like, alone at home, with Aunt Grace, in the summer. And, well, when Miss Barry came, I asked if she'd mind waiting a minute and . . ."

"You asked her to let Lisa come," Janie finished. She sat still, thinking it over. She added grudgingly, "I guess you couldn't do anything else, Pam. But I still think it's mean and Lisa's going to loathe it here. I know it right this minute. What did Tilly say when you asked her?"

"Well, that was queer, I thought," Pam answered slowly, remembering. "She said 'Lisa, eh? That's not the birthday present I had in mind for Janie exactly.' And then, she said, 'But if there is to be a balm in Gilead, I suppose we must let Lisa try to find it along with the rest of us. If we don't, we'll lose it ourselves.'"

"Oh," was all Janie could find to say.

She slid back down into her sleeping bag and curled up in the warmth. Pam was shivering. She began pulling off her sweatshirt.

"I wonder, though," Janie thought, looking out through the tent flap at the quiet frosty stars, "if Lisa will want the balm."

"Wear some wool socks to bed," she advised Pam abruptly.

Pam grunted assent and went headfirst into her dunnage bag to find a pair. Janie turned her head to watch her. Then she turned right over, away from Pam, and burrowed into her pillow.

When Dad had said she looked older that afternoon, she had been so sure that she really was. She had felt happier, wiser, nicer.

"One to grow on," Mother had said.

And, later, Janie had thought that that was what this time with Tilly had been — a time to grow on. Talking things over, reading, exploring, dreaming, living away from home, she had felt herself stretching up, getting ready to take the giant steps Tilly spoke of.

She wasn't ready, though. Lisa's coming had showed her that. She was as mixed-up, as hateful as ever. And she wasn't even sure she cared!

"Happy Birthday, dear Janie," she jeered, "Happy Birthday to you!"

She hoped that Pam could not tell that she was crying.

17

Make Way for Janie

JANIE wakened early. The sun had risen but there was still mist lying along the water. She could see that much from inside the tent. Cautiously, she inched out of her sleeping bag and pulled on her boots and her heavy sweater. Pam did not stir. Janie crept out and stood alone, breathing deeply, saying hello to the new day.

But it was still too cold to stay in one place. She trotted up to the privy Mr. Whitman had built for her and Tilly. She smiled when she saw it. She and Tilly, working together, had painted it green. It blended with the trees and bushes around it. Tilly had christened it "The Green House" and, whenever they needed to visit it, they would say casually, "I have to run up to the greenhouse for a moment." Tilly was a lover of even a poor pun, just like Dad.

When Janie came back, Tilly herself was out building

a fire. She looked up as her goddaughter came toward her. Her eyebrows raised in a silent question. Then she held out her arms. Janie went to her at once, although she moved quietly, not wanting to waken the other two girls.

"I guess I surprised you, Stephanie Jane," Tilly murmured with a grin. "I'm sure Pam explained."

"Yes, she did," Janie said. She hated to spoil Tilly's morning but she felt she should warn her. "I understand how you couldn't help asking her but, Tilly, she's going to hate it here."

"You don't hate it," Tilly stated. She did not need to ask.

"No, but I'm me. Lisa doesn't like reading much and she does like boys. I don't know what she'll *do!*"

Tilly frowned at the kindling in her hand. Then she gave a quick shrug.

"Wait and see, Janie. Let's give her a chance before we decide for her," she said. "Maybe Lisa isn't as grown-up as she pretends. And maybe I can help her find things to do. How would you like to finish making this fire while I go make a list?"

Janie built the fire carefully as Tilly had taught her. Out of the corner of her eye, though, she was watching her godmother. Tilly stole into the tent and emerged with her clipboard and a felt pen. With these and some paper, she disappeared to the far side of the Point.

An hour later, Pam and Lisa were up and the four of

them had finished breakfast. Tilly still had not mentioned her list. Janie was dying of curiosity but she contained herself.

"Now what do we do?" Lisa said fretfully as the last dish was put away in its orange crate.

"What would you like to do, Lisa?" Tilly asked.

"I don't know," Lisa said. "What is there to do in a place like this?"

"I'm glad you asked me that question," Tilly said smoothly — and produced her list. The three girls studied it. Even Janie's mouth was a little ajar as she saw the possibilities Tilly had dreamed up.

The list read:

> Swim
> Play croquet
> Knit
> Play cards
> Collect leaves
> Pick berries
> Hike
> Explore woods
> Read
> Write a letter
> Write a book
> Sketch
> Paint a picture

Play chess
Play tag
Get a tan
Clear out bigger sandy area for swimming
Sing
Climb a tree
Walk to country store (1½ miles)
Fish
Learn to canoe
Play Chinese checkers
Sew
Dream

"Gee, Tilly, that's quite a list," Janie spoke up finally.

"It's a start," was all Tilly said. "I'm sure we'll find things to add to it. I'm going to drive around to the Lodge up the lake and rent a canoe this morning. Pam, did you say you can't swim?"

"Yes," Pam said, hanging her head.

"It's nothing to be ashamed of when you haven't had a chance to learn," Tilly told her.

"I have my Senior Swimmer!" Lisa stared at Pam. "I was the youngest one in the class to get it, too," she bragged.

"Were you the youngest person in the class?" Tilly asked quietly.

Lisa nodded proudly.

"And did everyone earn them?"

"Yes."

"Then, of course you were the youngest one," Tilly said briskly. "Pam's going to be the youngest one in my class too. I don't guarantee she'll get her Senior Swimmer but I promise you she'll learn to swim."

Pam glowed. Janie wanted to hug Tilly but restrained herself.

"I have more news for you," Tilly went on. "You all know that I'm an artist."

They nodded. Janie had told them.

"Well, here I am in painter's heaven and I haven't even set up my easel," Tilly complained.

Janie had not once thought of that before. Tilly had seemed so happy, so busy — getting meals, tidying the tent, reading . . .

"I've been housekeeping and having a holiday," Tilly continued, not looking at Janie. "Now I'm going to give up housekeeping. You three are going to get all the meals from now on — and I am going to paint."

For once, they were united. The three of them wore identical dumbfounded expressions. Tilly snorted with laughter. She produced another list. It was horrifying. It listed which one of them was cook, which one did the cleaning up after the meal and which one took care of burning garbage and sweeping out the tents.

"Oh, it won't be that bad," Tilly comforted them. "You'll have lots of time left over to do other things. Besides, it's a lot more fun keeping house outside than in — and much easier too. Now who's coming with me to rent a boat? I think we'll make it a rowboat instead of a canoe. That way, Pam won't be so likely to drown. Till you learn to swim, though, Pam, you'll have to wear a life jacket at all times when you're in that boat and I don't want you to go out in it without me along."

Janie felt breathless. Things were happening so fast she hardly knew what to expect. Tilly was going to paint . . .

Of course, Tilly must have wanted to paint all along. And she'd probably like a tent to herself, too.

"Drat!" Janie said to herself.

She had known that ever since the night before but she had not let herself think it. There was plenty of room in the bigger tent for the three girls. That way, Tilly would be able to read at night the way Janie knew she loved to do.

"Well, are you coming with me or not?" Tilly demanded.

"Yes!"

"Sure!"

They sprang to their feet and were off ahead of her up the hill to the little car.

The boat was not too big for Janie to handle. It was

blue. It was an old boat but somebody had given it a new coat of paint and it looked as though it were waiting for Janie to come along and take it for a ride. Tilly made all the arrangements. She got life jackets.

Then she said casually, "Janie, you and Lisa will have to row it home if you want it. It's not far by water, only about half a mile. Here, I'll show you."

She began to point, and then checked herself.

"What am I doing?" she said. "All you have to do is follow the shore and you'll run right straight into the Point. Pam and I will beat you home and have the red carpet out."

"Okay," Janie said.

What else was there to say? Lisa looked longingly at the sleek canoes tied at the dock, but she said nothing. She did not even demand to row. She held onto the sides carefully and made her way to the stern. Janie clambered in after her and sat facing her.

"Don't let her row you onto a rock, Lisa," Tilly said as she and Pam started for the car.

Janie pulled on one oar, turned the rowboat carefully, and began to row for home. Lisa still said nothing. Her face looked strained, although perhaps it was only the sun shining on the water that made her seem to be frowning.

"Goodness," Janie thought, "this is the only time we've been alone together since that first afternoon when she came over after Sunday School."

That had been only a few weeks before. To Janie, now it seemed years ago.

"Keep out a bit," Lisa advised, "You're getting pretty close to shore. I can see the bottom."

Janie pulled on her right oar. Her arms were beginning to ache. They were not really hurting, just showing her that she needed to row more to build up some muscle.

"There's the Point, isn't it?" Lisa said, as they rounded a curve. Janie looked over her shoulder. She nodded and bent to her rowing again. But she had seen it. It had been just a glimpse, but now she could feel all its beauty, all its wonder, waiting for her. Her island, the island Tilly called hers, lay very still, dreaming and alone, waiting for her. The two tents gleamed in the sun. There were just two, but they gave the Point a gypsy look, as though magical things could happen there.

Two tents . . .

Janie hesitated. Then she thought "Gilead" — and she began to tell Lisa of her plan. Why couldn't the three girls sleep together in the bigger tent? That would give Tilly room to herself and it would be more fun for them too.

"There's even an extra orange crate we could move our books into," she wound up. By this time, a bookcase seemed as necessary to Janie as it did to Tilly.

Lisa's cheeks flushed. Her eyes brightened. A look, almost an eager look, flashed over her face. For one moment, she was the gay, lovely Lisa Janie had first seen. Then, her expression grew wary.

"That would be okay, I guess," she said listlessly, turning her head.

Janie kept right on rowing. Then Lisa straightened around and faced her again.

"One thing's sure though," she said, "I am a terrific cook. Our housekeeper taught me. I've never bothered with the kind of stuff your aunt has, though. I really cook — you know, pie and . . . and special casseroles. I haven't cooked ordinary camp food. Can you cook?"

Janie returned Lisa's look. In that instant, she knew that Lisa was still Lisa, that no magic was going to make the two of them into kindred spirits, that they were different kinds of people and always would be. She also knew that Lisa could not cook and was afraid to admit it.

A liar. That was what Lisa Daniels was.

It takes one to know one, Janie teased herself, in her inmost thoughts.

Her answer to Lisa, when it came, was spoken quietly, almost comfortingly.

"I'm a lousy cook," she said. "Once I even put sugar in the soup when Mother asked me to salt it. But I can learn — and so can you. Tilly'll teach us both. She'll never let us starve, that's for sure."

Lisa's smile came slowly. It was a new smile, not the gay, self-confident one the old Lisa had worn so lightly. This smile was shy and unsure and real.

"You didn't really put sugar in soup," Lisa said wonderingly.

Janie nodded vigorously.

"I did so," she said. "It was chicken soup, my father's favorite, and he took the first bite . . ."

"Oh, Janie," Lisa said.

Her smile broadened, stretched, grew to a grin. Then she began to laugh helplessly, idiotically. Tears came to her eyes. It was catching. Janie, too, snickered in spite of herself.

When Tilly shouted "Ship, ahoy!" Janie was laughing so hard that she crashed the boat into the shore with a resounding crunch.

"Janie, watch what you're doing!" Tilly shouted, grabbing for the rope.

Pam looked at the two girls in the boat. Their faces were crimson now. Tears had begun to roll down Janie's cheeks.

"What's so funny?" Pam asked.

"She . . . she . . . put sugar in her father's soup," Lisa gasped.

Janie, swaying with mirth, nodded foolishly.

"I did, Pam," she managed. "But I don't really know why it's so funny."

"Neither do I," said Tilly sharply.

She turned, then, in amazement. Pam, too, had exploded into a fit of giggles. She collapsed on the rocks at the water's edge and doubled over, chortling.

"You should just see yourselves," she gasped.

Shaking her head, Tilly left the three of them to it. She thought of the stiff Janie who had climbed into the boat half an hour before, of the unhappy, difficult Lisa who had been her reluctant passenger.

And now, this Janie! This Lisa!

How did she do it? Tilly marveled.

Somewhere, between the lodge and Gilead, Janie Chisholm had taken a giant step.

Tilly felt a sudden sharp longing to tell Janie she had seen the growth in her, not just in that one morning but through all the summer days that led to it. She wanted to let this girl she so loved know, by some special word or look, how proud she was of her at that moment. She hesitated, searching for a way to do it.

The girls' laughter had subsided now. Pam tied the boat securely. Lisa scrambled out onto the rock. Janie followed.

"Here comes the Chief Cook!" she bellowed suddenly, swashbuckling up the rocks toward Tilly. "Make room, Miss Barry. The Chief Cook is approaching. Stand to one side, *if* you please!"

"Make way for Janie!" Pam sang out, following Janie's lead.

Barefoot, wearing nothing but short shorts and a halter top, she managed to sweep along with all the airs and graces of a lady-in-waiting in court dress.

Lisa fell in at the end of the procession. Cupping her hands to form a trumpet, she blew an ear-splitting fanfare.

Watching them come, Tilly knew, all at once, that Janie did not need to be praised. She had discovered, inside herself, freedom and joy.

Janie was still shouting, drowning out the other two with her happy racket.

"Make way! Step aside, lady. Hotdogs à la Janie, coming up!"

Tilly did not say a word. She simply stood back and let them pass.